D0041296

Books by Meg Cabot

THE MEDIATOR 1: SHADOWLAND
THE MEDIATOR 2: NINTH KEY
THE MEDIATOR 3: REUNION
THE MEDIATOR 4: DARKEST HOUR
THE MEDIATOR 5: HAUNTED
THE MEDIATOR 6: TWILIGHT

THE PRINCESS DIARIES
THE PRINCESS DIARIES, VOLUME II: PRINCESS IN THE SPOTLIGHT
THE PRINCESS DIARIES, VOLUME III: PRINCESS IN LOVE
THE PRINCESS DIARIES, VOLUME IV: PRINCESS IN WAITING
THE PRINCESS DIARIES, VOLUME IV AND A HALF: PROJECT PRINCESS
THE PRINCESS DIARIES, VOLUME V: PRINCESS IN PINK
THE PRINCESS DIARIES, VOLUME VI: PRINCESS IN TRAINING
THE PRINCESS PRESENT: A PRINCESS DIARIES BOOK
PRINCESS LESSONS: A PRINCESS DIARIES BOOK
PERFECT PRINCESS: A PRINCESS DIARIES BOOK

ALL-AMERICAN GIRL
TEEN IDOL
NICOLA AND THE VISCOUNT
VICTORIA AND THE ROGUE
THE BOY NEXT DOOR
BOY MEETS GIRL
EVERY BOY'S GOT ONE

THE 1-800-WHERE-R-YOU BOOKS:
WHEN LIGHTNING STRIKES
CODE NAME CASSANDRA
SAFE HOUSE
SANCTUARY

MEG CABOT

the mediator
Twilight

HARPERCOLLINS*PUBLISHERS*

The author wishes to acknowledge that while she did live for a time in Carmel, California, and attended the Junipero Serra Mission School, she has taken liberties with certain other facts, including, but not exclusive to, making the Mission School a K–12 insitution, when in reality it educates only K–8, as well as inventing a hospital and sticking it in the middle of downtown Carmel-by-the-Sea. The author apologizes for any confusion these or other inaccuracies might cause to the residents of the area.

Twilight
Copyright © 2005 by Meg Cabot
All rights reserved. No part of this book may be used or reproduced in any manner whatsoever without written permission except in the case of brief quotations embodied in critical articles and reviews. Printed in the United States of America. For information address HarperCollins Children's Books, a division of HarperCollins Publishers, 1350 Avenue of the Americas, New York, NY 10019.

www.harperteen.com

Library of Congress Cataloging-in-Publication Data
Cabot, Meg.
   Twilight / Meg Cabot.— 1st U.S. ed.
     p. cm.
   Summary: Sixteen-year-old Carmel, California teenager Suze Simon is a typical high school student except for the fact that she is a "shifter" who can mediate between the living and the dead, and she is in love with a ghost from the nineteenth century.
   ISBN 0-06-072467-6 — ISBN 0-06-072468-4 (lib. bdg.)
   [1. Ghosts—Fiction. 2. Time travel—Fiction. 3. Death—Fiction. 4. High schools—Fiction. 5. Schools—Fiction. 6. Carmel (Calif.)—Fiction.] I. Title.
PZ7.C211165Tw 2004
[Fic]—dc22   2004010138
                                                   CIP
                                                   AC

Typography by Sasha Illingworth
1 2 3 4 5 6 7 8 9 10
❖
First Edition

For Benjamin

Acknowledgments

Many thanks to Beth Ader, Jennifer Brown, Laura Langlie, Abigail McAden, and especially Benjamin Egnatz, as well as all of the readers who supported this series from the beginning.

It had been a typical Saturday morning in Brooklyn. Nothing out of the ordinary. Nothing to make me suspect it was the day my life was going to change forever. Nothing at all.

I'd gotten up early to watch cartoons. I didn't mind getting up early if it meant I'd get to spend a few hours with Bugs and his friends. It was getting up early for school that I resented. Even back then, I hadn't been too fond of school. My dad had to tickle my feet on weekdays to get me out of bed.

Not on Saturdays, though.

I think my dad felt the same. About Saturdays, I mean. He was always the first one out of bed in our apartment, but he got up extra early on Saturdays, and instead of oatmeal with brown sugar, which he made me for breakfast on weekdays, he made French toast. My mom, who'd never been able to stomach the smell of maple syrup, always stayed in bed until our breakfast plates had been rinsed and put in the dishwasher, and all of the counters were wiped down, and the smell was gone.

That Saturday—the one right after I turned six—my dad and I had cleaned up the syrupy dishes and counters, and then I'd returned to cartoons. I can't remember which one I'd been watching when my dad strode in to tell me good-bye, but it had been a good enough one that I'd wished he'd hurry up and leave already.

"I'm going running," he'd said, planting a kiss on the top of my head. "See ya, Suze."

"Bye," I'd said. I don't think I even bothered to look at him. I knew what he looked like. A big tall guy with a lot of thick dark hair that had gone white in some places. That day, he'd been wearing gray jogging pants and a T-shirt that read HOMEPORT, MENEMSHA, FRESH SEAFOOD ALL YEAR ROUND, left over from our last trip to Martha's Vineyard.

Neither of us had known then they'd be the last clothes anyone would ever see him in.

"Sure you don't want to come to the park with me?" he'd asked.

"Da-ad," I'd said, appalled at the thought of missing a minute of cartoons. "No."

"Suit yourself," he'd said. "Tell your mom there's fresh-squeezed orange juice in the fridge."

"Okay," I said. "Bye."

And he'd left.

Would I have done anything differently, if I'd known it was the last time I'd ever see him again—alive, anyway? Of course I would have. I would have gone to the park with him.

I'd have made him walk, instead of run. If I'd known he was going to have a heart attack out there on the running path and die in front of strangers, I'd have stopped him from going to the park in the first place, made him go to the doctor instead.

Only I hadn't known. How could I have known?

How could I?

chapter *one*

I found the stone exactly where Mrs. Gutierrez had said it would be, beneath the drooping branches of the overgrown hibiscus in her backyard. I shut off the flashlight. Even though there was supposed to have been a full moon that night, by midnight a thick layer of clouds had blown in from the sea, and a dank mist had reduced visibility to nil.

But I didn't need light to see by anymore. I just needed to dig. I sunk my fingers into the wet soft earth and pried the stone from its resting spot. It moved easily and wasn't heavy. Soon I was feeling beneath it for the tin box Mrs. Gutierrez had assured me would be there. . . .

Except that it wasn't. There was nothing beneath my fingers except damp soil.

That's when I heard it—a twig snapping beneath the weight of someone nearby.

I froze. I was trespassing, after all; the last thing I needed was to be dragged home by the Carmel, California, cops.

Again.

Then, with my pulse beating frantically as I tried to figure out how on earth I was going to explain my way out of this one, I recognized the lean shadow—darker than all the others—standing a few feet away. My heart continued to pound in my ears, but now for an entirely different reason.

"You," I said, climbing slowly, shakily, to my feet.

"Hello, Suze." His voice, floating toward me through the mist, was deep, and not at all unsteady . . . unlike my own voice, which had an unnerving tendency to shake when he was around.

It wasn't the only part of me that shook when he was around, either.

But I was determined not to let him know that.

"Give it back," I said, holding out my hand.

He threw back his head and laughed.

"Are you nuts?" he wanted to know.

"I mean it, Paul," I said, my voice steady, but my confidence already beginning to seep away, like sand beneath my feet.

"It's two thousand dollars, Suze," he said, as if I might be unaware of that fact. "Two *thousand*."

"And it belongs to Julio Gutierrez." I sounded sure of myself, even if I wasn't exactly feeling that way. "Not you."

"Oh, right," Paul said, his deep voice dripping with sarcasm. "And what's Gutierrez gonna do, call the cops? He doesn't know it's missing, Suze. He never even knew it was there."

"Because his grandmother died before she had a chance

to tell him," I reminded him.

"Then he won't notice, will he?" Despite the darkness, I could tell Paul was smiling. I could hear it in his voice. "You can't miss what you never knew you had."

"Mrs. Gutierrez knows." I'd dropped my hand so he wouldn't see it shaking, but I couldn't disguise the growing unsteadiness in my voice as easily. "If she finds out you stole it, she'll come after you."

"What makes you think she hasn't already?" he asked, so smoothly that the hairs on my arms stood up . . . and not because of the brisk autumn weather, either.

I didn't want to believe him. He had no reason to lie. And obviously, Mrs. Gutierrez had come to him as well as me, anxious for any help she could get. How else could he have known about the money?

Poor Mrs. Gutierrez. She had definitely put her trust the wrong mediator. Because it looked as if Paul hadn't just robbed her. Oh, no.

But like a fool, I stood there in the middle of her back-yard and called her name just in case, as loudly as I dared. I didn't want to wake the grieving family inside the modest stucco home a few yards away.

"Mrs. Gutierrez?" I craned my neck, hissing the name into the darkness, trying to ignore the chill in the air . . . and in my heart. "Mrs. Gutierrez? Are you there? It's me, Suze. . . . Mrs. Gutierrez?"

I wasn't all that surprised when she didn't show. I knew, of course, that he could make the undead disappear. I just never thought he'd be low enough to do it.

I should have known better.

A cold wind kicked up from the sea as I turned to face him. It tossed some of my long dark hair around my face until the strands finally ended up sticking to my lip gloss. But I had more important things to worry about.

"It's her life savings," I said to him, not caring if he noticed the throb in my voice. "All she had to leave to her kids."

Paul shrugged, his hands buried deep in the pockets of his leather jacket.

"She should have put it in the bank, then," he said.

Maybe if I reason with him, I thought. Maybe if I explain . . . "A lot of people don't trust banks with their money—"

But it was no use.

"Not my fault," he said with another shrug.

"You don't even need the money," I cried. "Your parents buy you whatever you want. Two thousand dollars is nothing to you, but to Mrs. Gutierrez's kids, it's a fortune!"

"She should have taken better care of it, then," was all he said.

Then, apparently seeing my expression—though I don't know how, since the clouds overhead were thicker than ever—he softened his tone.

"Suze, Suze, Suze," he said, pulling one of his hands from his jacket pocket and moving to drape his arm across my shoulders. "What am I going to do with you?"

I didn't say anything. I don't think I could have spoken if I'd tried. It was hard enough just to breathe. All I could think about was Mrs. Gutierrez, and what he'd done to her. How could someone who smelled so good—the sharp clean scent of his cologne filled my senses—or from whom such warmth radiated—especially welcome, given the chill in the air and the relative thinness of my windbreaker—be so . . .

Well, evil?

"Tell you what," Paul said. I could feel his deep voice reverberating through him as he spoke, he was holding me that close. "I'll split it with you. A grand for each of us."

I had to swallow down something—something that tasted really bad—before I could reply. "You're sick."

"Don't be that way, Suze," he chided. "You have to admit, it's fair. You can do whatever you want with your half. Mail it back to the Gutierrezes, for all I care. But if you're smart, you'll use it to buy yourself a car now that you finally got your license. You could put a down payment on a decent set of wheels with that kind of change, and not have to worry about sneaking your mom's car out of the driveway after she's fallen asleep—"

"I hate you," I snapped, twisting out from beneath his grip and ignoring the cold air that rushed in to meet the place where his body had been warming mine.

"No, you don't," he said. The moon appeared momentarily from behind the blanket of clouds overhead, just long enough for me to see that his lips were twisted into a lop-sided grin. "You're just mad because you know I'm right."

I couldn't believe my ears. Was he serious? "Taking money from a dead woman is the right thing to do?"

"Obviously," he said. The moon had disappeared again, but I could tell from his voice that he was amused. "She doesn't need it anymore. You and Father Dom. You're a couple of real pushovers, you know. Now I've got a question for you. How'd you know what she was blathering about, anyway? I thought you were taking French, not Spanish."

I didn't answer him right away. That's because I was frantically trying to think of a reply that wouldn't include the word I least liked uttering in his presence, the word that, every time I heard it or even thought it, seemed to cause my heart to do somersaults over in my chest, and my veins to hum pleasantly.

Unfortunately, it was a word that didn't exactly engender the same response in Paul.

Before I could think of a lie, however, he figured it out on his own.

"Oh, right," he said, his voice suddenly toneless. "*Him.* Stupid of me."

Then, before I could think of something to say that would lighten the situation—or at least get his mind off Jesse, the last person in the world I wanted Paul Slater to be thinking about—he said in quite a different tone, "Well, I don't know about you, but I'm beat. I'm gonna call it a night. See you around, Simon."

He turned to go. Just like that, he turned to go.

I knew what I had to do, of course. I wasn't looking forward to it . . . in fact, my heart had pretty much slipped up into my throat, and my palms had gone suddenly, inexplicably damp.

But what choice did I have? I couldn't let him walk away with all that money. I'd tried reasoning with him, and it hadn't worked. Jesse wouldn't like it, but the truth was, there was no other alternative. If Paul wouldn't give up the money voluntarily, well, I was just going to have to take it from him.

I told myself I had a pretty good chance at succeeding, too. Paul had the box tucked into the inside pocket of his jacket. I'd felt it there when he'd put his arm around me. All I had to do was distract him somehow—a good blow to the solar plexus would probably do the job—then grab the box and chuck it through the closest window. The Gutierrezes would freak, of course, at the sound of the breaking glass, but I highly doubted they'd call the cops . . . not when they found two thousand bucks scattered across the floor.

As plans went, it wasn't one of my best, but it was all I had.

I called his name.

He turned. The moon chose that moment to slip out from behind the thick veil of clouds overhead, and I could see by its pale light that Paul wore an absurdly hopeful expression. The hopefulness increased as I slowly crossed the grass between us. I suppose he thought for a minute that he'd finally broken me down. Found my weakness. Successfully lured me to the dark side.

And all for the low, low price of a thousand bucks.

Not.

The hopeful look left his face, though, the second he noticed my fist. I even thought that, just for a moment, I caught a look of hurt in his blue eyes, pale as the moonlight around us. Then the moon moved back behind the clouds, and we were once again plunged into darkness.

The next thing I knew, Paul, moving more quickly than I would have thought possible, had seized my wrists in a grip that hurt and kicked my feet out from under me. A second later, I was pinned to the wet grass by the weight of his body with his face just inches from mine.

"That was a mistake," he said, way too casually, considering the force with which I could feel his heart hammering against mine. "I'm rescinding my offer."

His breath, unlike my own, wasn't coming out in ragged gasps, though. Still, I tried to hide my fear from him.

"What offer?" I panted.

"To split the money. I'm keeping it all, now. You really hurt my feelings, you know that, Suze?"

"I'm sure," I said as sarcastically as I could. "Now get off me. These are my favorite low-riders, and you're getting grass stains on them."

But Paul wasn't ready to let me go. He also didn't appear to appreciate my feeble attempt to make a joke out of the situation. His voice, hissing down at me, was deadly serious.

"You want me to make your boyfriend disappear," he asked, "the way I did Mrs. Gutierrez?"

His body was warm against mine, so there was no other explanation for why my heart went suddenly cold as ice, except that his words terrified me to the point that my blood seemed to freeze in my veins.

I couldn't, however, let my fear show. Weakness only seems to trigger cruelty, not compassion, from people like Paul.

"We have an agreement," I said, my tongue and lips forming the words with difficulty because they, like my heart, had gone ice cold with dread.

"I promised I wouldn't kill him," Paul said. "I didn't say anything about keeping him from dying in the first place."

I blinked up at him, uncomprehending.

"What . . . what are you talking about?" I stammered.

"You figure it out," he said. He leaned down and kissed me lightly on my frozen lips. "Good night, Suze."

And then he stood up and vanished into the fog.

It took me a minute to realize I was free. Cool air rushed in to all the places where his body had been touching mine. I finally managed to roll over, feeling as if I'd just suffered a head-on collision with a brick wall. Still, I had enough strength left to call out, "Paul! Wait!"

That's when someone inside the Gutierrez household flicked on the lights. The backyard lit up bright as an airport runway. I heard a window open and someone shout, "Hey, you! What are you doing there?"

I didn't stick around to ask whether or not they planned on calling the cops. I peeled myself up from the ground and ran for the wall I'd scaled a half hour ago. I found my mom's car right where I'd left it. I hopped into it and started my long journey home, cursing a certain fellow mediator—and the grass stains on my new jeans—the whole way.

I had no idea that night how bad things were going to get between Paul and me.

But I was about to find out.

chapter two

He'd done it. Finally. Just like, deep down, I guess I'd always known he would.

You would think, what with everything I'd been through, I'd have seen it coming. I'm not exactly new at this. And it wasn't as if all the warning signs hadn't been there.

Still, the blow, when it came, seemed to strike like a bolt out of the clear blue.

"So where are you going for dinner before the Winter Formal?" Kelly Prescott asked me in fourth period language lab. She didn't even wait to hear what my answer was. Because Kelly didn't care what my answer was. That wasn't the point of her asking me in the first place.

"Paul's taking me to the Cliffside Inn," Kelly went on. "You know the Cliffside Inn, don't you, Suze? In Big Sur?"

"Oh, sure," I said. "I know it."

That's what I said, anyway. Isn't it weird how your brain can slip into autopilot? Like, how you can be saying one thing and thinking something entirely different? Because when Kelly said that—about Paul taking her to the Cliffside Inn—the first thing I thought wasn't *Oh, sure, I know it.* Not even close. My first thought was more along the lines of *What? Kelly Prescott? Paul Slater is taking KELLY PRESCOTT to the Winter Formal?*

But that's not what I said out loud, thank God. I mean, considering that Paul himself was sitting just a few study carrels away, futzing with the sound on his tape player. The last thing in the world I wanted was for him to think I was, you know, peeved that he'd asked someone else to the formal. It was bad enough that he noticed I was even looking in his direction, let alone talking about him. He raised his eyebrows all questioningly, as if to say, "May I be of service?"

That's when I saw he still had on his headphones. He hadn't, I realized with relief, heard what Kelly had said. He'd been listening to the scintillating conversation between Dominique and Michel, our little French friends.

"It got five stars," Kelly went on, settling into her carrel. "The Cliffside Inn, I mean."

"Cool," I said, resolutely ripping my gaze from Paul's and pulling out the chair to my own carrel. "I'm sure you two will have a really great time."

"Oh, yeah," Kelly said. She flipped her honey-blonde hair back so she could slip on her headphones. "It'll be so romantic. So where're you going? To eat before the dance, I mean."

She knew, of course. She knew perfectly well.

But she was going to make me say it. Because that's

how girls like Kelly are.

"I guess I'm not going to the dance," I said, sitting down at the carrel beside hers and putting on my own head-phones.

Kelly looked over the partition between us, her pretty face twisted with sympathy. Fake sympathy, of course. Kelly Prescott doesn't care about me. Or anyone, except herself.

"Not going? Oh, Suze, that's terrible! Nobody asked you?"

I just smiled in response. Smiled and tried not to feel Paul's gaze boring into the back of my head.

"That's too bad," Kelly said. "And it looks like Brad's not going to be able to go, either, what with Debbie being out with mono. Hey, I've got an idea." Kelly giggled. "You and Brad should go to the dance together!"

"Funny," I said, smiling weakly as Kelly tittered at her own joke. Because, you know, there isn't anything quite as pathetic as a girl being taken to the junior–senior Winter Formal by her own stepbrother.

Except, possibly, her not being taken by anyone at all.

I turned on my tape player. Dominique immediately began to complain to Michel about her *dormitoire*. I'm sure Michel murmured sympathetic replies (he always does), but I didn't hear what they were.

Because it didn't make any sense. What had just hap-pened, I mean. How could Paul be taking Kelly to the Winter Formal when, last time I'd checked, *I* was the one he was hounding for a date . . . any date? Not that I'd been especially thrilled about it, of course. But I did have to throw him the occasional bone, if only to keep him from doing to my boyfriend what he'd done to Mrs. Gutierrez.

Wait a minute. Was *that* what was going on? Paul was finally getting tired of hanging around with a girl he had to blackmail into spending time with him?

Well, good. Right? I mean, if Kelly wanted him, she could have him.

The only problem was, I was having a hard time not remembering the way Paul's body had felt as it had lain across mine that night in the Gutierrezes' yard. Because it had felt good—his weight, his warmth—despite my fear. Really good.

Right sensation . . . wrong guy.

But the right guy? Yeah, he wasn't a real pin-the-girl-to-the-grass kind of person. And warmth? He hadn't given off any in a century and a half.

Which wasn't his fault, really. The warmth thing, I mean. Jesse couldn't help being dead any more than Paul could help being . . . well, Paul.

Still, this asking-Kelly-and-not-me-to-the-dance thing . . . it was freaking me out. I'd been bracing myself for his invitation—and his reaction to my turning it down—for weeks. I'd even begun thinking I was finally getting the hang of the back-and-forth nature of our relationship . . . as if it were a tennis game at the resort where we'd met last summer.

Except that now I had a sinking feeling that Paul had just lobbed a ball into my court that I was never going to be able to hit back.

What was that all about?

The words floated before my eyes, scrawled on a piece of paper torn from a notebook, and were waved at me from over the top of the wooden partition separating my carrel from the one in front of it. I pulled the piece of paper from the fingers clutching it and wrote, *Paul asked Kelly to the Winter Formal*, then slid the page over the partition.

A few seconds later, the paper fluttered back down in front of me.

I thought he was going to ask you!!! my best friend, CeeCee, wrote.

I guess not, I scribbled in response.

Well, maybe it's just as well, was CeeCee's reply. *You didn't want to go with him, anyway. I mean, what about Jesse?*

But that was just it. What *about* Jesse? If Paul had asked me to the Winter Formal, and I'd responded with something less than enthusiasm to his invitation, he'd let loose one of his cryptic threats about Jesse—the newest one, in fact, about him apparently having learned of some way to keep the dead from having passed on in the first place. . . . Whatever that meant.

And yet today he'd turned around and asked someone else to go to the dance with him instead. Not just someone else, either, but Kelly Prescott, the prettiest, most popular girl in school . . . but also someone I happened to know Paul despised.

Something wasn't right about any of this . . . and it wasn't just that I was trying to save all my dances for a guy who's been dead for 150-odd years.

But I didn't mention this to CeeCee. Best friend or no, there's only so much a sixteen-year-old girl—even a sixteen-year-old albino who happens to have a psychic aunt—can understand. Yes, she knew about Jesse. But Paul? I hadn't breathed a word.

And I wanted to keep it that way.

Whatever, I scrawled. *How about you? Adam ask you yet?*

I looked around to make sure Sister Marie-Rose, our French teacher, wasn't watching before I slid the note back toward CeeCee, and instead spotted Father Dominic waving at me from the language lab doorway.

I removed my headphones with no real regret—Dominique's and Michel's whining would hardly have been riveting in English; in French, it was downright unbearable—and hurried to the door. I felt, rather than saw, that a certain gaze was very much on me.

I would not, however, give him the satisfaction of glancing his way.

"Susannah," Father Dominic said as I slipped out of the language lab and into one of the open breezeways that served as hallways between classrooms at the Junipero Serra Mission Academy. "I'm glad I was able to catch you before I left."

"Left?" It was only then that I noticed Father D. was holding an overnight bag and wearing an extremely anxious expression. "Where are you going?"

"San Francisco." Father Dominic's face was nearly as white as his neatly trimmed hair. "I'm afraid something terrible has happened."

I raised my eyebrows. "Earthquake?"

"Not exactly." Father Dominic pushed his wire-rimmed spectacles into place at the top of his perfectly aquiline nose as he squinted down at me. "It's the monsignor. There's been an accident and he's in a coma."

I tried to look suitably upset, although the truth is, I've never really cared for the monsignor. He's always getting upset about stuff that doesn't really matter—like girls who wear miniskirts to school. But he never gets upset over stuff that's actually important, like how the hot dogs they serve at lunch are always stone-cold.

"Wow," I said. "So what happened? Car crash?"

Father Dominic cleared his throat. "Er, no. He, um, choked."

"Somebody strangled him?" I asked hopefully.

"Of course not. Really, Susannah," Father Dom chided me. "He choked on a piece of hot dog at a parish barbecue."

Whoa! Poetic justice! I didn't say so out loud, though, since I knew Father Dom wouldn't approve.

Instead, I said, "Too bad. So how long will you be gone?"

"I have no idea," Father Dom said, looking harassed. "This couldn't have happened at a worse time, either, what with the auction this weekend."

The Mission Academy is ceaseless in its fund-raising efforts. This weekend the annual antique auction would be taking place. Donations had been flooding in all week and were being stashed for safekeeping in the rectory basement. Some of the more notable items that the booster club had received included a turn-of-the-century Ouija board (courtesy of CeeCee's psychic aunt, Pru) and a silver belt buckle—estimated by the Carmel Historical Society to be more than 150 years old—discovered by my stepbrother, Brad, while he was cleaning out our attic, a task assigned to him as punishment for an act of malfeasance, the nature of which I could no longer recall.

"But I wanted to make sure you knew where I was." Father Dominic plucked a cell phone from his pocket. "You'll call me if anything, er, out of the ordinary occurs, won't you, Susannah? The number is—"

"I know the number, Father D.," I reminded him. Father Dom's cell phone was new, but not *that* new. May I just add that it totally sucks that Father Dominic, who has never wanted—nor has the slightest idea how to use—a cell phone has one and I don't? "And by out of the ordinary, do you mean stuff like Brad getting a passing grade on his trig midterm, or more supernatural phenomena, like ectoplasmic manifestations in the basilica?"

"The latter," Father Dom said, pocketing the cell phone again. "I hope not to be gone for more than a day or two, Susannah, but I am perfectly aware that in the past it hasn't taken much longer than that for you to get yourself into mortal peril. Kindly, while I'm away, see to it that you exercise a modicum of caution in that capacity. I don't care to return home, only to find another section of the school blown to kingdom come. Oh, and if you would, make sure that Spike has enough food—"

"Nuh-uh," I said, backing away. It was the first time in a

long time that my wrists and hands were free of angry red scratches, and I wanted to keep it that way. "That cat's your responsibility now, not mine."

"And what am I to do, Susannah?" Father D. looked frustrated. "Ask Sister Ernestine to look in on him from time to time? There aren't even supposed to be pets in the rectory, thanks to her severe allergies. I've had to learn to sleep with the window open so that that infernal animal can come and go as it pleases without being spotted by any of the novices—"

"Fine," I interrupted him, sighing gustily. "I'll stop by PETCO after school. Anything else?"

Father Dominic pulled a crumpled list from his pocket.

"Oh," he said after skimming it. "And the Gutierrez funeral. All taken care of. And I've put the family on our neediest-case roster, as you requested."

"Thanks, Father D.," I said quietly, looking away through the arched openings in the breezeway toward the fountain in the center of the courtyard. Back in Brooklyn, where I'd grown up, November meant death to all flora. Here in California—even though it's northern California— all November apparently means is that the tourists, who visit the Mission daily, wear khakis instead of Bermuda shorts, and the surfers down on Carmel Beach have to exchange their short-sleeved wetsuits for long-sleeved ones. Dazzling red and pink blossoms still fill the Mission's flower beds, and when we're released for lunch each noon, it's still possible to work up a sweat under the sun's rays.

Still, temperatures in the seventies or not, I shivered . . .

and not just because I was standing in the cool shade of the breezeway. No, it was a cold that came from inside that was causing the goose bumps on my upper arms. Because, beautiful as the Mission gardens were, there was no denying that beneath those glorious petals lurked something dark and . . .

. . . well, Paul-like.

It was true. The guy had the ability to cause even the brightest day to cloud over. At least, as far as I was concerned. Whether or not Father Dominic felt the same, I didn't know . . . but I kind of doubted it. After his somewhat rocky start to the school year, Paul had ended up not having nearly as much regular contact with the school principal as I did. Which, given that all three of us are mediators, might seem a little strange.

But both Paul and Father D. seem to like it that way, each preferring to keep his distance, with me as a go-between when communication is absolutely necessary. This was partly because they were—let's face it—guys. But it was also because Paul's behavior—at school, anyway—had improved considerably, and there was no reason for him to be sent to the principal's office. Paul had become a model student, making impressive grades and even getting appointed captain of the Mission Academy men's tennis team.

If I hadn't seen it for myself, I wouldn't have believed it. But there it was. Obviously, Paul preferred to keep Father D. in the dark about his after-school activities, knowing that the priest was hardly likely to approve of them.

Take the Gutierrez incident, for instance. A ghost had come to us for help and Paul, instead of doing the right thing, had ended up stealing two thousand dollars from her. This was not something Father Dominic would have turned a blind eye to, had he known about it.

Only he didn't know about it. Father D., I mean. Because Paul wasn't about to tell him, and, frankly, neither was I. Because if I did—if I told Father Dominic anything that might make Paul seem less than the straight-A-getting jock he was pretending to be—what had happened to Mrs. Gutierrez was going to happen to my boyfriend.

Or, you know, the guy who would be my boyfriend. If he weren't dead.

Paul had me, all right. Right where he wanted me. Well, maybe not exactly *right* where he wanted me, but close enough. . . .

Which was why I'd had to resort to subterfuge in order to secure some form of justice for the Gutierrezes, who'd been robbed, even if they didn't know it. I couldn't go to the police, of course (*Well, you see, officer, Mrs. Gutierrez's ghost told me the money was hidden beneath a rock in her backyard, but when I got there, I found out another mediator had taken it. . . .What's a mediator, you ask? Oh, a person who acts as a liaison between the living and the dead. Hey, wait a minute . . . what're you doing with that strait jacket?*).

Instead, I'd placed the family's name on the Mission's neediest list, which had secured Mrs. Gutierrez a decent funeral and enough money for her loved ones to pay off some of her debt. Not two thousand dollars' worth, though, that was for sure. . . .

"—while I'm gone, Susannah."

I tuned in to what Father Dominic was saying to me a little too late. And I couldn't ask, *What was that, Father D.?* Because then he'd want to know what I'd been thinking about, instead of paying attention to what he was saying.

"Do you promise, Susannah?"

Father Dominic's blue-eyed gaze bore into mine. What could I do but swallow and nod?

"Sure, Father D.," I said, not having the slightest idea what I was promising.

"Well, I must say, that makes me feel better," he said, and it was true that his shoulders seemed to lose some of the rigidity with which he'd been holding them as we'd talked. "I know, of course, that I can trust the two of you. It's just that . . . well, I would hate for you to do anything— er, stupid—in my absence. Temptation is difficult enough for anyone to resist, particularly the young, who haven't fully considered the consequences of their actions."

Oh. Now I knew what he'd been talking about.

"But for you and Jesse," Father Dominic went on, "there would be especially catastrophic repercussions should the two of you happen to, er—"

"—give in to our unbridled lust for each other?" I suggested when he trailed off.

Father Dominic eyed me unhappily.

"I'm serious, Susannah," he said. "Jesse doesn't belong in this world. With any luck, he won't continue to remain here for much longer. The deeper the attachment you form for each other, the more difficult it's going to be to say good-bye. Because you will have to say good-bye to him one day, Susannah. You can't defy the natural order of—"

Blah blah blah. Father D's lips were moving, but I tuned him out again. I didn't need to hear the lecture again. So things hadn't worked out for Father Dominic and the girl-ghost he'd fallen in love with, way back in the Middle Ages. That didn't mean Jesse and I were destined to follow the same path. Especially not considering what I'd managed to pick up from Paul, who seemed to know a good deal more than Father Dom did about being a mediator . . .

. . . particularly the little-known fact that mediators can bring the dead back to life.

There was just one little fly in the ointment: You needed to have a body to put the wrongfully deceased's soul into. And bodies aren't something I happen to stumble across on a regular basis. At least, not ones willing to sacrifice the soul currently occupying them.

"Sure thing, Father Dom," I said as his speech petered out at last. "Listen, have a real good time in San Francisco."

Father Dominic grimaced. I guess people who are going to San Francisco to visit comatose monsignors don't necessarily get a lot of time off for touristy stuff like visiting the Golden Gate Bridge or Chinatown or whatever.

"Thank you, Susannah," he said. Then he pinned me with a meaningful stare. *"Be good."*

"Am I ever anything but?" I asked with some surprise.

He walked away, shaking his head, without even bothering to reply.

chapter *three*

"So what were you and the good father gabbing about during lab today?" Paul wanted to know.

"Mrs. Gutierrez's funeral," I replied truthfully. Well, more or less. I've found it doesn't pay to lie to Paul. He has an uncanny ability to discover the truth on his own.

Not, of course, that it means what I tell him is the strictest truth. I just don't practice a policy of full disclosure where Paul Slater is concerned. It seems safer that way.

And it definitely seemed safer not to let Paul know that Father Dominic was in San Francisco, with no known date of return.

"You're not still upset about that, are you?" Paul asked. "The Gutierrez woman, I mean? The money's going to good use, you know."

"Oh, sure, I know," I said. "Dinner at the Cliffside Inn's got to run, what, a hundred a plate? And I assume you'll be renting a limo."

Paul smiled at me lazily from the pillows he was leaning against.

"Kelly told you?" he asked. "Already?"

"First chance she got," I said.

"Didn't take her long," he said.

"When did you ask her? Last night?"

"That's right."

"So about twelve hours," I said. "Not bad, if you consider that for about eight of them, she was probably sleeping."

"Oh, I doubt that," Paul said. "That's when they do their best work. Succubuses, I mean. I bet Kelly only needs an hour or two of shut-eye a night, tops."

"Romantic." I turned a page of the crusty old book lying between us on Paul's bed. "Calling your date for the Winter Formal a succubus, I mean."

"At least she *wants* to go with me," Paul said, his face expressionless—with the exception of a single dark brow, which rose, almost imperceptibly, higher than the one next to it. "A refreshing change, I must say, from the usual state of things around here."

"You hear me complaining?" I asked, turning another page. I prided myself that I was maintaining—outwardly, anyway—a supremely indifferent attitude about the whole thing. Inside, of course, it was a whole other story. Because inside, I was screaming, *What's going on? Why'd you ask Kelly and not me? Not that I care about the stupid dance, but just what game do you think you're playing now, Paul Slater?*

It was amazing how none of this showed, however. At least, so far as I knew.

"It's just that I'd have appreciated some advance notice that I'd been stricken from the agenda," was what I said aloud. "For all you knew, I might have already blown a fortune on a dress."

One corner of Paul's mouth flicked upward.

"You hadn't," Paul said. "And you weren't going to, either."

I looked away. It was hard to meet his gaze sometimes, it was so penetrating, so . . .

Blue.

A strong, tanned hand came down over mine, pinning my fingers to the page I'd been about to turn.

"That's the one." Paul doesn't seem to have the same problem looking into my eyes (probably because mine are green and about as penetrating as, um, algae) that I have looking into his. His gaze on my face was unwavering. "Read it."

I looked down. The book Paul had pulled out for our latest "mediator lesson" was so old, the pages had a tendency to crumble beneath my fingers as I turned them. It belonged in a museum, not a seventeen-year-old guy's bedroom.

But that was exactly where it had ended up, pulled— though I doubted Paul knew I was aware of it—from his grandfather's collection. *The Book of the Dead* was what it was called.

And the title wasn't the only reminder that all things have an expiration date. It smelled as if a mouse or some other small creature had gotten slammed between the pages some time in the not-so-distant past, left to slowly decompose there.

"'If the 1924 translation is to be believed,'" I read aloud, glad my voice wasn't shaking the way I knew my fingers were—the way my fingers always shook when Paul touched me—"'the shifter's abilities didn't merely include communication with the dead and teleportation between their world and our own, but the ability to travel at will throughout the fourth dimension, as well.'"

I will admit, I didn't read with a lot of feeling. It wasn't exactly a barrel of laughs, going to school all day, then having to go to mediation tutoring. Granted, it was only once a week, but that was more than enough, believe me. Paul's house hadn't lost any of its sterility in the months I'd been coming to it. If anything, the place was as creepy as ever . . .

. . . and so was Paul's grandfather, who continued to live what he'd described, in his own words, as a "half-life," in a room down the hall from Paul's. That half-life seemed to be made up of around-the-clock health attendants, hired to see to the old man's many ailments, and incessant viewing of the Game Show Network. It isn't any wonder, really, that Paul avoids Mr. Slater—or Dr. Slaski, as the good doctor himself had confided to me he was really named—like the plague. His grandfather isn't exactly scintillating company, even when he isn't pretending to be loopy due to his meds.

Despite my less-than-inspired performance, however, Paul released my hand and leaned back once more, looking extremely pleased with himself. "Well?" Another raised eyebrow.

"Well, what?" I flipped the page, and saw only a copy of the hieroglyph they were talking about.

The half smile Paul had been wearing vanished. His face was as expressionless as the wall behind him.

"So that's how you're going to play it," he said.

I had no idea what he was talking about. "Play what?" I asked.

"I could do it, Suze," he said. "It can't be hard to figure out. And when I do . . . well, you won't be able to accuse me of not having stuck by our agreement."

"What agreement?"

Paul set his jaw.

"Not to kill your boyfriend," he said tonelessly.

I just stared at him, genuinely taken aback. I had no idea where this was coming from. We'd been having a perfectly nice—well, okay, not nice, but ordinary—afternoon, and all of a sudden he was threatening to kill my boyfriend . . . or not to kill him, actually. What was going on?

"Wh-what are you talking about?" I stammered. "What does this have to do with Jesse? Is this . . . is this because of the dance? Paul, if you'd asked, I'd have gone with you. I don't know why you turned around and asked Kelly without even—"

The half grin came back, but this time, all Paul did was lean forward and flip the book closed. Dust rose from the ancient pages, almost right up into my face, but I didn't complain. Instead, I waited, my heart in my throat, for him to reply.

I was destined for disappointment, however, since all he

said was, "Don't worry about it," then swung his legs over the side of the bed and stood up. "You hungry?"

"Paul." I followed him, my Stuart Weitzmans clacking loudly on the bare tile floor. "What's going on?"

"What makes you think anything's going on?" he asked as he made his way down the long, shiny hallway.

"Oh, gee, I don't know," I said, fear making me sound waspish. "That crack you made the other night about Jesse. And letting me off the hook for the Winter Formal. And now this. You're up to something."

"Am I?" Paul glanced up at me as he made his way down the spiral staircase to the kitchen. "You really think so?"

"Yes," I said. "I just haven't figured out what yet."

"Do you have any idea what you sound like right now?" Paul asked as he pulled open the Sub-Zero refrigerator and peered inside.

"No," I said. "What?"

"A jealous girlfriend."

I nearly choked. "And how *are* things on Planet You Wish?"

He found a can of Coke and cracked it open.

"Nice one," he said in reference to my remark. "No, really. I like that. I might even use it myself someday."

"Paul." I stared at him, my throat dry, my heart banging in my chest. "What are you up to? Seriously."

"Seriously?" He took a long swig of soda. I couldn't help noticing how tanned his throat was as I watched him swallow. "I'm hedging my bets."

"What does *that* mean?"

"It means," he said, closing the refrigerator door and leaning his back against it, "that I'm starting to like it around here. Strange, but true. I never thought of myself as the captain-of-the-tennis-team type. God knows, at my last school"—he took another long pull at the soda—"Well, I won't get into that. The truth is, I'm starting to get into this high school stuff. I want to go to the Winter Formal. Thing is, I figure you won't want to be around me for a while, after I . . . well, do what I plan on doing."

He'd closed the refrigerator door, so that couldn't have been what caused the sudden chill I felt all along my spine. He must have seen me shiver, since he went, with a grin, "Don't worry, Susie. You'll forgive me eventually. You'll realize, in time, that it's all for the be—"

He didn't get to finish. That's because I'd strode forward and knocked the Coke can right out of his hand. It landed with a clatter in the stainless-steel sink. Paul looked down at his empty fingers in some surprise, like he couldn't figure out where his drink had gone.

"I don't know what you're planning, but let me make one thing clear: If anything happens to him," I hissed, not much louder than the soda fizzing from the can in the sink, but with a lot more force, "anything at all, I will make you regret the day you were born. Understand?"

The look of surprise on his face twisted into one of grim annoyance.

"That wasn't part of our deal. All I said was that I wouldn't—"

"*Anything*," I said. "And don't call me Susie."

My heart was banging so loudly inside my chest that I didn't see how he couldn't hear it—how he couldn't see that I was more frightened than I was angry. . . .

Or maybe he did, since his lips relaxed into a smile—the same smile that had made half the girls in school fall madly in love with him.

"Don't worry, Suze," he said. "Let's just say that my plans for Jesse? They're a lot more humane than what you've got planned for me."

"I—"

Paul just shook his head. "Don't insult me by pretending like you don't know what I mean."

I didn't have to pretend. I had no idea what he was talking about. I didn't get a chance to tell him that, though, because at that moment a side door opened, and we heard someone call, "Hello?"

It was Dr. Slaski, along with his attendant, back from one of their endless rounds of doctor's appointments. The attendant was the one who'd let out the greeting. Dr. Slaski—or Slater, as Paul referred to him—never said hello. At least, not when anybody but me was around.

"Hey," Paul said, going out into the living room and looking down at his wheelchair-bound grandfather. "How'd it go?"

"Just fine," the attendant said with a smile. "Didn't it, Mr. Slater?"

Paul's grandfather said nothing. His head was slumped down onto his chest, as if he were asleep.

Except that he wasn't. He was no more asleep than I

was. Inside that battered and frail-looking exterior was a mind crackling with intelligence and vitality. Why he chose to hide that fact, I still don't understand. There's a lot about the Slaters that I don't understand.

"Your friend staying for dinner, Paul?" the attendant asked cheerfully.

"Yes," Paul said at the same time I said, "No."

I didn't meet his gaze as I added, "You know I can't."

This, at least, was true. Mealtime is family time at my house. Miss one of my stepfather's gourmet dinners, and you'll never hear the end of it.

"Fine," Paul said through teeth that were obviously gritted. "I'll take you home."

I didn't object. I was more than ready to go.

Our ride should have been a lot more enjoyable than it was. I mean, Carmel is one of the most beautiful places in the world, and Paul's grandfather's house is right on the ocean. The sun was setting, seeming to set the sky ablaze, and you could hear waves breaking rhythmically against the rocks below. And Paul, who isn't exactly painful to look at, doesn't drive any old hand-me-down car, either, but a silver BMW convertible that I happen to know I look extremely good in, with my dark hair, pale skin, and excellent taste in footwear.

But you could have cut the tension inside that car with a knife, nonetheless. We rode in utter silence until Paul finally pulled up in front of 99 Pine Crest Drive, the rambling Victorian house in the Carmel hills that my mother and stepfather had bought more than a year ago, but still hadn't finished refurbishing. Seeing as how it had been built at the turn of the century—the nineteenth, not the twentieth—it needed a lot of refurbishing. . . .

But no amount of recessed lighting could rid the place of its violent past, or the fact that, a few months earlier, they'd dug up my boyfriend's skeleton from the backyard. I still couldn't set foot on the deck without feeling nauseated.

I was about to get out of the car without a word when Paul reached over and put a hand on my arm.

"Suze," he said, and when I turned my head to look at him, I saw that his blue eyes looked troubled. "Listen. What would you say to a truce?"

I blinked at him. Was he kidding? He'd threatened to off my boyfriend; stole from people he'd been asked to help; and neglected to invite me to the school dance, humiliating me in front of the most popular girl in the whole school in the process. And now he wanted to kiss and make up?

"Forget it," I said as I gathered up my books.

"Come on, Suze," he said, flashing me that heart-melting smile. "You know I'm harmless. Well, basically. Besides, what could I do to your boy Jesse? He's got Father D. to protect him, right?"

Not really. Not now, anyway. But Paul didn't know that. Yet.

"I'm sorry about the thing with Kelly," he said. "But you didn't want to go with me. Can you blame me for wanting to take someone who . . . well, actually likes me?"

Maybe it was the smile. Maybe it was the way he blinked those baby blues. I don't know what it was, but suddenly, I found myself softening toward him.

"What about the Gutierrezes?" I asked. "You'll give the money back?"

"Uh," Paul said. "Well, no. I can't do that."

"Paul, you can. I won't tell, I swear. . . ."

"It's not that. I can't because . . . I, er, need it."

"For *what*?"

Paul grinned. "You'll find out."

I threw open the car door and got out, my heels sinking deep into the pine-needle-strewn lawn.

"Good-bye, Paul," I said, and slammed the door behind me, cutting off his "No, Suze, wait!"

I turned around and headed toward the house. My stepfather, Andy, had started a fire in one of the house's many fireplaces. The rich smell of burning wood filled the crisp evening air, tinged with the scent of something else. . . .

Curry. It was tandoori chicken night. How could I have forgotten?

Behind me, I heard Paul throw the car into reverse and drive away. I didn't look back. I headed up the stairs to the front door, stepping into the squares of light thrown onto the porch from the living room windows. I opened the door and went inside, calling "I'm home!"

Except that I wasn't, really. Because home meant something else to me now, and had for quite a while.

And he didn't live there anymore.

chapter *four*

The handful of pebbles I'd thrown rattled noisily against the heavy, leaded glass. I looked around, worried someone might have heard. But better for them to hear tiny rocks hitting a window than me whispering the name of someone who wasn't even supposed to be living there. . . .

Someone who, technically speaking, wasn't living at all.

He appeared almost at once, not at the window, but by my side. That's the thing about the undead. They never have to worry about the stairs. Or walls.

"Susannah." The moonlight threw Jesse's features into high relief. There were dark pools in the place where his eyes should have been, and the scar in his eyebrow—a dog bite wound from childhood—showed starkly white.

Still, even with the tricks the moon was playing, he was the best-looking thing I had ever seen. I don't think it's just the fact that I'm madly in love with him that makes me think so, either. I'd shown the miniature portrait of him I'd accidentally-on-purpose snagged from the Carmel Historical Society to CeeCee, and she'd agreed. *Hottie extraordinaire* was how she'd put it, to be exact.

"You don't have to bother with these," he said, reaching out to brush the remaining pebbles from my hand. "I knew you were here. I heard you calling."

Except, of course, that I hadn't. Called him. But whatever. He was here now and that's what mattered.

"What is it, Susannah?" Jesse wanted to know. He'd moved out of the shadows of the rectory, so that I could finally see his eyes. As usual, they were darkly liquid and full of intelligence . . . intelligence, and something else. Something, I like to think, that's just for me.

"Just stopped by to say hi," I said with a shrug. It was chilly enough that when I spoke, I could see my breath fog up in front of me.

This didn't happen when Jesse spoke, however. Because, of course, he has no breath.

"At three in the morning?" The dark eyebrows shot up, but he looked more amused than alarmed. "On a school night?"

He had me there, of course.

"Father D. asked me to pick up some cat food," I said, brandishing a bag. "I didn't want Sister Ernestine to see me smuggling it in. She's not supposed to know about Spike."

"Cat food," Jesse said. Now he *definitely* looked amused. "Is that all?"

It wasn't all and he knew it. But it also wasn't what he thought. At least, not exactly.

Still, when he pulled me toward him, I didn't precisely object. Especially not considering that there's only one place in the world I feel completely safe anymore, and that's where I was just then . . . in his arms.

"You're cold, *querida*," he whispered into my hair. "You're shivering."

I was, but not because I was cold. Well, not *only* because I was cold. I closed my eyes, melting in his embrace as I always did, reveling in the feel of his strong arms around me, his hard chest beneath my cheek. I wished I could have stayed that way forever—in Jesse's arms, I mean—where nothing could ever hurt me. Because he'd never let it.

I don't know how long we stood like that in the vegetable garden behind the rectory where Father Dom lived. All I know is that eventually Jesse, who'd been stroking my hair, pulled back a little, so that he could look down into my face.

"What is it, Susannah?" he asked me again, his voice sounding strangely rough, considering the tenderness of the moment. "What's wrong?"

"Nothing," I lied, because I didn't want it to end . . . the moonlight, his embrace, any of it . . . all of it.

"Not nothing," he said, reaching up and pulling a strand of hair from where the wind had blown it, so that it was sticking to my lip gloss. I always seem to have that problem. "I know you, Susannah. I know there's something the matter. Come."

He took me by the hand and pulled. I went with him, even though I didn't know where we were going. I'd have followed him anywhere, even into the bowels of hell. Only of course he'd never take me there.

Unlike some people.

I did balk a little when I saw where he had led me, though. It wasn't exactly hell, but . . .

"The *car*?" I stared at the hood of my mom's Honda Accord.

"You're cold," Jesse said firmly, opening the driver's side door for me. "We can talk inside."

Talking wasn't really what I'd had in mind. Still, I figured we could do what I *had* had in mind just as easily in the car as in the rectory's vegetable garden. And it *would* be a lot warmer.

Only Jesse wasn't having any of it. He seized both my hands as I tried to slip them around his neck, and placed them firmly in my lap.

"Tell me," he said from the shadows of the passenger seat, and I could tell by his voice that he was in no mood for games.

I sighed and stared out the windshield. As far as romance went, this was not exactly what I'd call a prime make-out spot. Big Sur, maybe. The Winter Formal, definitely. But the rectory parking lot at the Junipero Serra Mission? Not so much.

"What is it, *querida*?" He reached out to sweep back some of my hair, which had fallen over my face.

When he saw my expression, however, he pulled his hand back.

"Oh. *Him*," he said in an entirely different voice.

I guess I shouldn't have been surprised. That he'd known, I mean, without my having said anything. There was just so much I hadn't told Jesse—so much that I'd decided I didn't dare tell him. My agreement with Paul, for instance: that, in return for Paul not removing Jesse to the great beyond, I'd meet with him after school every Wednesday under the auspices of learning more about our unique skill . . . although truthfully, most of the time it seemed all Paul wanted to do was get his tongue in my mouth, not study mediator lore.

Jesse would not have been particularly enthused had he known of the lessons . . . less so, if he'd had an inkling of what they actually entailed. There was no love lost between Jesse and Paul, whose relationship had been rocky from the start. Paul seemed to think he was superior to Jesse merely because he happened to be alive and Jesse was not, while Jesse disliked Paul because he'd been born with every priv-ilege in the world—including the ability to communicate with the dead—and yet chose to use his gifts for his own selfish purposes.

Of course, their mutual disdain for each other might also have had something to do with me.

Back before Jesse had come into my life, I used to sit around and fantasize about how great it would be to have two guys fighting over me. Now that it was actually happen-ing, though, I realized what a fool I'd been. There was noth-ing funny about the grounding I'd gotten the last time the two of them had gone at it, destroying half the house in the process. And that fight hadn't even been my fault. Much.

"It's just," I said, careful not to meet his gaze because I knew if I looked into those twin dark pools I'd be lost, as usual, "Paul's been . . . worse than usual."

"Worse?" The glance Jesse shot me was stiletto sharp. "Worse in what way? Susannah, if he's laid a hand on you—"

"Not that," I interrupted quickly, realizing with a sinking heart that the speech I'd been up half the night rehearsing—the speech that I'd convinced myself was so perfect, I needed to hurry right down to the rectory to say it now, at once, even though it was the middle of the night and I'd have to "borrow" my mom's car to get there—wasn't perfect at all. . . . In fact, it was completely wrong. "What I mean is, lately, he's been threatening . . . well, to do something I don't really understand. To you."

Jesse looked amused. Which was not exactly the reaction I'd been expecting.

"So you came rushing down here," he said, "in the middle of the night to warn me? Susannah, I'm touched."

"Jesse, I'm serious," I said. "I think Paul's up to something. Remember Mrs. Gutierrez?"

"Of course." Jesse had translated the dead woman's frantic message for me because my Spanish is pretty much confined to *taco* and, of course, *querida*. "What about her?"

Quickly, I told him about having met Paul in Mrs. Gutierrez's backyard. Even though I skimmed over the bit about Paul having stolen the money before I'd been able to get my hands on it, Jesse's outrage was obvious. I saw a glint of steel in his eyes, and he said something in Spanish that I couldn't understand, but I'm guessing it wasn't complimentary to Paul's parentage.

"Father D.'s going to take care of it," I hastened to assure him, in case Jesse was getting any ideas about trying to take Paul on—something I'd warned him repeatedly would be foolhardy in the extreme. I didn't say that Father D. was unaware of Paul's theft . . . only that the Gutierrezes were in need. I knew what Jesse would say if he found out I'd left Father Dominic in the dark about Paul's latest transgression.

I also knew, however, what Paul would do if he found out I'd narced on him.

"But that's not what I'm worried about," I added hastily. "It's something Paul said when I . . . when I tried to get him to give the money back." I thought it better to leave out the part about when I'd gone for Paul's solar plexus. Also the thing Paul had said earlier in the day, about how his plans for Jesse were more humane than my own plans for himself. Because I had a feeling now that I knew what he'd meant by that. Though he couldn't have been more wrong. "It was something about you and what he was going to do you. Not kill you—"

"That," Jesse interrupted dryly, "would be difficult, *querida*, given that I'm already dead."

I glared at him. "You know what I mean. He said he *wasn't* going to kill you. He was going to . . . I think he said he was going to keep you from having died in the first place."

Even in the darkness of the car's interior, I saw Jesse's eyebrow go up.

44

"He has a very high opinion of his own abilities, that one" was all he said, however.

"Jesse," I said. I couldn't believe he wasn't taking Paul's threat seriously. "He really meant it. He's said it to me a couple of times, now. I seriously think he might be up to something."

"Slater is always going to be up to something where you're concerned, Susannah," Jesse said, in a voice that suggested he was more than a little tired of the subject. "He's in love with you. Ignore him, and eventually he'll go away."

"Jesse," I said. I couldn't, of course, tell him that I'd have liked nothing better than to turn my back on Paul and his manipulative ways, but that I couldn't because I'd promised him I wouldn't . . . in return for Jesse's life. Or at least his continued presence in this dimension. "I really think—"

"Ignore him, Susannah." Jesse was smiling a little now as he shook his head. "He's only saying these things because he knows they upset you, and then you pay attention to him. *'Oh, Paul! No, don't, Paul!'*"

I looked at him in horror. "Was that supposed to be an imitation of *me*?"

"Don't gratify him by paying attention," Jesse continued as if he hadn't heard me, "and he'll grow tired of it and move on."

"I don't sound anything like that." I chewed my lower lip uncertainly. "Do I really sound like that?"

"And now, if that's all," Jesse went on, ignoring me exactly the way he'd told me to ignore Paul, "I think you should be getting home, *querida*. If your mother should wake and find you gone, you know she'll worry. Besides, don't you have school in a few hours?"

"But—"

"*Querida.*" Jesse leaned over the gearshift and slipped a hand behind my neck. "You worry too much."

"Jesse, I—"

But I didn't get to finish what I'd started to say—nor, a second later, could I even recall what I'd meant to tell him. That's because he'd pulled me—gently, but inexorably— toward him, and covered my mouth with his.

Of course, it's impossible when Jesse's lips are on mine to think about anything other than the way those lips make me feel . . . which is unbelievably cherished and desired. I don't have a whole lot of experience in the kissing depart- ment, but even I know that what happens every time Jesse kisses me is . . . well, extraordinary.

And not just because he's a ghost, either. All the guy has to do is lower his lips to mine and it's like a Fourth of July sparkler going off deep inside me, flaming brighter and brighter until I can hardly bear the white-hot heat any- more. The only thing that seems as if it might put the fire out is pressing myself closer to him. . . .

But, of course, that only makes it worse, because then Jesse—who usually seems to have a fire of his own burning somewhere—ends up touching me someplace, beneath my shirt, for instance, where, of course, I *want* to be touched, but where he doesn't think his fingers have any business roaming. Then the kissing ends as Jesse apologizes for insulting me, even though insulted is the *last* thing I feel, something I've made as clear to him as I can, to no apparent avail.

But that's what I get for falling in love with a guy who was born back when men still treated women as if they were dainty breakable figurines instead of flesh and blood. I've tried to explain to him that things are different now, but he remains stubbornly convinced that everything below the neck is off-limits until the honeymoon. . . .

Except, of course, when we're kissing, like now, and he happens, in the heat of the moment, to forget he's a nineteenth-century gentleman.

I felt his hand move along the waistband of my jeans as we kissed. Our tongues entwined, and I knew it was only a matter of time until that hand slipped beneath my sweater and up toward my bra. I uttered a giddy prayer of thanks that I'd worn the front-closing one. Then, my eyes closed, I did a little exploration of my own, running my palms along the hard wall of muscles I could feel through the cotton of his shirt . . .

. . . until Jesse's fingers, instead of dipping inside my 34 B, seized my hand in a grip of iron.

"Susannah." He was breathing hard and the word came out sounding a little ragged as he rested his forehead against mine.

"Jesse." I wasn't breathing too evenly myself.

"I think you'd better go now."

How had I known he was going to say that?

It occurred to me that we would be able to do this—kiss

like this, I mean—a lot more often and more conveniently if Jesse would get over the absurd idea that he has to stay with Father Dominic, now that we are, for want of a better word, an item. It was my bedroom, after all, that he'd been murdered in, way back when. Shouldn't it be my bedroom he continues to haunt?

I didn't couch it in those terms, though, since I knew Jesse, who's an old-fashioned guy, doesn't exactly approve of couples living together before wedlock. I also put resolutely from my mind the warning Father Dominic had given me, just before he'd left for San Francisco, about not giving into temptation where Jesse is concerned. It's all very well for Father D. to talk. He's a *priest*. He has no idea what it's like to be a red-blooded teenage mediator. Of the female variety.

"Jesse," I said, still a little breathless from all the kissing, "I can't help thinking . . . well, this thing with Paul. I mean, who knows if maybe he really has come up with some new way to . . . to keep you and me apart? And now, with Father Dom gone for who knows how long, I . . . . Well, don't you think it might be better if you came back to my house for a while?"

Jesse, even though he'd almost just had his hand up my shirt, didn't like that idea at all. "So you can protect me from the nefarious Mr. Slater?" Was it my imagination or did he sound more amused than, er, aroused? "Thank you for the invitation, *querida*, but I can take care of myself."

"But if Paul finds out Father D. is gone, he might come

after you. And if I'm not around to stop him—"

"This may come as a surprise to you, Susannah," Jesse said, lifting his head and placing my hand in my lap once more, "but I can handle Slater without your help."

Now he *definitely* sounded amused.

"And now you're going home," he went on. "Good night, *querida*."

He kissed me one last time, a brief peck good-bye. I knew that any second he was going to disappear.

But there was still something else I needed to know. Ordinarily, I'd have asked Father Dominic, but since he wasn't around . . .

"Wait," I said. "Before you go . . . one last thing."

Jesse had already started to shimmer. "What, *querida*?"

"The fourth dimension," I blurted out.

He had begun to dematerialize, but now he looked solid again.

"What about it?" he asked.

"Um," I said. I'm sure he thought I was just asking to keep him there for a few more precious seconds. And truthfully? I probably was. "What is it?"

"Time," Jesse said.

"Time?" I echoed. "That's it? Just . . . time?"

"Yes," Jesse said. "Time. Why do you ask? For school?"

"Sure," I said. "For school."

"The things they teach now," he said, shaking his head.

"Cat food," I said, holding out the bag. "Don't forget."

No wonder we can't seem to make it past second base.

He took the bag from me.

"Good night, *querida*," he said.

And then he was gone. The only sign that he'd been there at all were the badly fogged windows, steamed by our breath.

Or rather, by my breath, since Jesse doesn't have any.

chapter *five*

Mr. Walden held up a stack of Scantron sheets and said, "Number-two pencils only, please."

Kelly Prescott's hand immediately shot up into the air.

"Mr. Walden, this is an outrage." Kelly takes her role as president of the junior class extremely seriously . . . especially when it has to do with scheduling dances. And, apparently, aptitude testing. "We should have been given at least twenty-four hours' notice that we'd be undergoing state testing today."

"Relax, Prescott." Mr. Walden, our homeroom teacher and class advisor, began passing out the Scantron sheets. "They're career aptitude tests, not academic. Your scores won't show up on your permanent record. They're to help you"—he picked up one of the test booklets lying on his desk and read from it aloud—"'determine which careers are best suited to your particular skills and/or areas of interest and/or achievement.' Got it? Just answer the questions."

Mr. Walden slapped a pile of answer sheets onto my desk for me to pass down my row. "You've got fifty minutes. And no talking."

"'Which do you enjoy more, working while a) outdoors? or b) indoors?'" I heard my stepbrother Brad read aloud from across the room. "Hey, where's c) heavily intoxicated?"

"You loser,'" Kelly Prescott chortled.

"'Are you a 'night person' or a 'day person'?" Adam McTavish looked mockly shocked. "This test is totally biased against narcoleptics."

"'Do you work best a) alone or b) in a group?'" My best friend, CeeCee, could hardly seem to contain her disgust. "Oh my God, this is *so stupid*."

"What part of 'no talking,'" Mr. Walden demanded, "do you people not understand?"

But no one paid any attention to him.

"This *is* stupid," Adam declared. "How is this test going to determine whether or not I'm qualified for a career?"

"It measures your *aptitude*, stupid." Kelly sounded disgusted. "The only career you're qualified for is working the drive-through window at In-N-Out Burger."

"Where you, Kelly, will be working the fryer," Paul pointed out dryly, causing the rest of the class to crack up. . . .

Until Mr. Walden, who'd settled behind his desk and was trying to read his latest issue of *Surf Magazine*, roared, "Do you people want to stay after school to finish up those tests? Because I'll be happy to keep you here; I've got nothing better to do. Now, shut up, all of you, and get to work."

That had a significant impact on the amount of chitchat going on around the room.

Miserably, I filled in the little bubbles. My misery didn't just stem, of course, from the fact that I was operating on zero sleep. While that didn't exactly help, there was the more pressing concern than career aptitude tests. Yeah, they don't much apply to me. My fate is already laid out for me . . . has been laid out for me since birth. I'm destined to be one thing when I grow up and one thing only. And any other career I choose is just going to get in the way of my true calling, which is, of course, helping the undead to their final destinations.

I glanced over at Paul. He was bent over his Scantron sheet, filling in the answer bubbles with a little smile on his face. I wondered what he was putting down as fields of interest. I hadn't noticed any entries for extortion. Or felony theft.

Why, I wondered, was he even bothering? It wasn't like it was going to do us any good. We were always going to be mediators first, whatever other careers we might choose. Look at Father Dominic. Oh sure, he had managed to keep his mediator status a secret . . . a secret even from the church, since, as Father D. put it, his boss is God, and God invented mediators.

Of course, Father D. isn't *just* a priest. He'd also been a teacher for years and years, winning some awards, even, until he'd been promoted to principal.

But it's different for Father Dom. He really believes that

his ability to see and speak to the dead is gift from God. He doesn't see it for what it really is: a curse.

Except . . . except, of course, that without it, I never would have met Jesse.

Jesse. The little blank bubbles in front of me grew decidedly blurry as my eyes filled up with tears.

Oh, great. Now I was crying. At *school*.

But how could I help it? Here I was, my future laid out in front of me . . . graduation, college, career. Well, you know, pseudo-career, since we all know what my *real* career was going to be.

But what about Jesse? What future did *he* have?

"What's wrong with you?" CeeCee hissed.

I reached up and dabbed at my eyes with the sleeve of my Miu Miu shirt. "Nothing," I whispered back. "Allergies."

CeeCee looked skeptical, but turned back to her test booklet.

I'd asked him once what he'd wanted to be. Jesse, I mean. You know, before he'd died. I'd meant what he'd wanted to be as a far as a career went, but he hadn't understood. When I'd finally explained, he'd smiled but in a sad way.

"Things were different when I was alive, Susannah," he'd said. "I was my father's only son. It was expected that I would inherit our family's ranch and work it to support my mother and sisters after my father died."

He didn't add that part of the plan had also included his marrying the girl whose dad owned the farm next door, so that their land would be united into one supersized ranchero. Nor did he mention the fact that she was the one who'd had him killed, because she'd liked another fella better, a fella her dad hadn't exactly approved of. Because I already knew all of that.

Things were tough, I guess, even way back in the 1850s.

"Oh," was what I'd said in response. Jesse hadn't spoken with any detectable rancor, but it seemed like a raw deal to me. I mean, what if he hadn't *wanted* to be a rancher? "Well, what would you have *liked* to be? You know, if you'd had a choice?"

Jesse had looked thoughtful. "I don't know. It was different then, Susannah. *I* was different. I did think . . . sometimes . . . that I might have liked to have been a doctor."

A doctor. It made perfect sense—at least to me. All those times I'd staggered home with various parts of me throbbing in pain—whether from poison oak or blisters on my feet—Jesse had been there for me, his touch soft as cashmere. He'd have made a great doctor, actually.

"Why didn't you, then?" I'd wanted to know. "Become a doctor? Just because of your dad?"

"Yes, mostly that," he'd said. "I'd never even dared mention it to anyone. I could barely be spared from the ranch for a few days, let alone the years medical school would have taken. But I would have liked that, I think. Medical school. Though back when I was alive," he'd added, "people didn't know nearly as much about medicine as they do today. It would be more exciting to work in the sciences now, I think."

And he would know. He'd had 150 years to hang around

and watch as inventions—electricity, automobiles, planes, computers . . . not to mention penicillin and vaccines for diseases that in the past had routinely killed millions— changed the world into something unrecognizable from the one in which he'd grown up.

But rather than clinging stubbornly to the past, as some would have, Jesse had followed along excitedly, reading whatever he could get his hands on, from paperback novels to encyclopedias. He said he had a lot to catch up on. His favorite books seem to be the nonfiction tomes he borrows from Father Dom, everything from philosophy to explorations on emerging viruses—the kind of books I'd have given to my dad on Father's Day, if my dad wasn't, you know, dead. My stepdad, on the other hand, is more the cookbook type. But you get my drift. To Jesse, stuff that seems dry and uninteresting to me is vitally exciting. Maybe because he'd seen it all unfolding before his eyes.

Sighing, I looked down at the hundreds of career options in front of me. Jesse was dead, but even *he* knew what he'd wanted to be . . . would have been, if he hadn't died. Or not been, considering what he'd said about his father's expectations for him.

And here I was, with every advantage in the world, and all I could think that I wanted to be when I grew up was . . .

Well, with Jesse.

"Twenty more minutes." Mr. Walden's voice boomed out across the classroom, startling me from my thoughts. I found that my gaze had become fixed on the sea less than a mile from the Mission and viewable through most of the school's classroom windows . . . to the detriment of students like me. I hadn't grown up, like most of my classmates, around the sea. It was a constant source of wonder and interest to me.

Kind of, I realized, like Jesse's fascination with modern science.

Only unlike Jesse, I actually had a chance to *do* something with my interest.

"Ten more minutes," Mr. Walden announced, startling me again.

Ten more minutes. I looked down at my answer sheet, which was half empty. At the same time, I noticed CeeCee shooting me an anxious look from her desk beside mine. She nodded to the sheet. *Get to work*, her violet eyes urged me.

I picked up my pencil and began to haphazardly fill in bubbles. I didn't care what answers I chose. Because, truthfully, I didn't care about my future. Without Jesse, I *had* no future. Of course, with him, I had no future, either. What was he going to do, anyway? Follow me to college? To my first job? My first apartment?

Yeah. That'll happen.

Paul was right. I'm so stupid. Stupid to have fallen in love with a ghost. Stupid to think we had any kind of future together. Stupid.

"Time's up." Mr. Walden pulled his feet from the top of his desk. "Lay your pencils down, please. Then pass your answer sheets to the front."

I wasn't all that surprised when Paul came up to me

after Mr. Walden had dismissed us for lunch. "That was pointless," he said in a low voice, as we made our way toward our lockers. "I mean, we have our career paths cut out for us, don't we?"

"Well, you can't really make a living doing what we do," I said, then remembered, too late, that Paul certainly seemed to have managed to.

"An *honest* living," I amended.

But instead of feeling ashamed of himself, as I'd meant him to, Paul just grinned.

"That's why I've decided on a career in the legal profession," he said. "Your dad was a lawyer, right?"

I nodded. I don't like talking about my dad with Paul. Because my dad was everything that was good. And Paul is everything that . . . isn't.

"Yeah, that's what I thought," Paul went on. "Nothing's black and white with the law. It's all sort of gray. So long as you can find a precedent."

I didn't say anything. I could easily see Paul as a lawyer. Not a lawyer like my dad had been, a public defender, but the kind of lawyer who'd defend rich celebrities, people who thought they were above the law . . . and because they had limitless funds to pay for their defense, they *were* above it, in a way.

"You, on the other hand," Paul said. "I think you're destined for a career in the social services. You're a natural-born do-gooder."

"Yeah," I said, as I stopped beside my locker. "Maybe I'll follow in Father D.'s footsteps, and become a nun."

"Now that," Paul said, leaning against the locker next to mine, "would just be a waste. I was thinking more along the lines of a social worker. Or a therapist. You're very good, you know, at taking on other people's problems."

Wasn't that the truth? It was the reason I was so bleary-eyed and tired today. Because after I'd left Jesse the night before, I'd driven home and gone up to bed . . . only not to sleep. Instead, I'd lain awake, blinking at the ceiling and mulling over what Jesse had told me. Not about Paul, but about what Paul had made me read aloud earlier that day: *The shifter's abilities didn't merely include communication with the dead and teleportation between their world and our own, but the ability to travel at will throughout the fourth dimension as well.*

The fourth dimension. Time.

The very word caused the hairs on my arms to stand up, even though it was another typically beautiful autumn day in Carmel and not cold at all. Could it really be true? Was such a thing even possible? Could mediators—or shifters, as Paul and his grandfather insisted on calling us—travel through time as well as between the realms of the living and the dead?

And if—a big if—it *were* true, what on earth did it *mean*?

More important, why had Paul been so intent on making sure I knew about it?

"You look strung out," Paul observed as I stowed my books away and reached for the paper bag containing the lunch my stepfather had made me: tandoori chicken salad. "What's the matter? Trouble sleeping?"

59

"You should know," I said, glaring at him.

"What'd *I* do?" he asked, sounding genuinely surprised.

I don't know if it was my exhaustion, or the fact that that the career aptitude test had got me thinking about my future . . . my future and Jesse's. Suddenly, I was just very tired of Paul and his games. And I decided to call him on the latest one.

"The fourth dimension," I reminded him. "Time travel?"

He just grinned, however. "Oh, good, you figured it out. Took you long enough."

"You really think shifters are capable of time travel?" I asked.

"I don't think so," Paul said. "I *know* so."

Again, I felt a chill when I shouldn't have. We were standing in the shade of the breezeway, it was true, but just a few feet away in the Mission courtyard, the sun was blazing down. Hummingbirds flitted from hibiscus blossom to hibiscus blossom. Tourists snapped away with their digital cameras.

So what was up with the goose bumps?

"Why?" I demanded, my throat suddenly dry. "Because you've done it?"

"Not yet," he said, casually. "But I will. Soon."

"Yeah," I said, fear making me sarcastic. "Well, maybe you could travel back to the night you stole Mrs. Gutierrez's money and *not* do it this time."

"God, would you let it go already?" He shook his head. "It was two thousand lousy bucks. You act like it was two million."

"Hey, Paul." Kelly Prescott broke away from her

clique—the Dolce and Gabbana Nazis as CeeCee had taken to calling them—and sauntered over, fluttering her heavily mascaraed eyelashes. "You coming to lunch?"

"In a minute," Paul said to her . . . not very nicely, considering she was his date for next weekend's dance. Kelly, though stung, nevertheless pulled herself together enough to send me a withering glance before heading for the yard where we dined daily, al fresco.

"So I don't get it." I stared at him. "What if we *can* travel through time? Big deal. It's not like we can *change* anything once we get there."

"Why?" Paul's blue eyes were curious. "Because Doc from *Back to the Future* said so?"

"Because you can't . . . you can't mess up the natural order of things," I said.

"Why not? Isn't that what you do every day when you mediate? Aren't you interfering with the natural order of things by sending spirits off to their just reward?"

"That's different," I said.

"How so?"

"Because those people are already dead! They can't do anything that might change the course of history."

"Like Mrs. Gutierrez and her two thousand dollars?" Paul's glance was shrewd. "You think if you'd given it to her son, it wouldn't have changed the course of history? Even in some small way?"

"But that's different than entering another dimension to change something that already happened. That's just . . . wrong."

"Is it, Suze?" A corner of Paul's mouth lifted. "I don't think so. And you know what? I think this time, your boy Jesse is going to agree. With me."

And suddenly, it seemed to get even colder than ever under that breezeway.

chapter *six*

Please be home, please be home, please be home, I prayed as I waited for someone to answer the doorbell. *Please please please please . . .*

I don't know if someone heard my prayer, or if it was just that invalid archeologists don't get out that much. In any case, Dr. Slaski's attendant answered the front door, recognition dawning when he saw that it was me who'd been ringing the bell with so much urgency.

"Oh hi, Susan," he said, getting the name wrong, but the face that went with it right. Sort of. "You looking for Paul? Because far as I know, he's still in school—"

"I know he's still at school," I said, stepping hurriedly inside the Slaters' foyer, before the attendant could close the door. "I'm not here to see him. I stopped by to see his grandfather, if that's all right."

"His *grandfather*?" The attendant looked surprised. And why shouldn't he? For all he knew, his patient hadn't had a lucid conversation with anyone in years.

Except that he had. And it had only been a few months ago. With me.

"You know, Susan, Paul's grandpa isn't . . . he's not real well," the assistant said slowly. "We don't like to talk about it in front of him, but his last round of tests . . . Well, they didn't look so good. In fact, the doctors aren't giving him all that much longer to live. . . ."

"I just need to ask him a question," I said. "Just one little question. It'll only take a second."

"But . . ." The attendant, a young guy who, judging from his sun-bleached dreads, probably used whatever spare time he got to hit the waves, scratched his chin. "I mean, he can't . . . he doesn't really talk all that much anymore. The Alzheimer's, you know . . ."

"Can I just try?" I asked, not caring that I sounded like a whacko. I was *that* desperate. Desperate for answers that I knew only one person on earth could give me. And that person was just right upstairs. "Please? I mean, it couldn't hurt, could it?"

"No," the attendant said slowly. "No, I guess it couldn't hurt."

"Great," I said, slipping past him and starting up the stairs two at a time. "I'll just be a couple of minutes. You won't mind leaving us alone, will you? I'll call you if he looks like he might need you."

The attendant, closing the front door in a distracted sort of way, went, "Okay. I guess. But . . . shouldn't you be in school?"

"It's lunchtime," I informed him cheerfully, as I made my way up the stairs and then down the hall toward Dr. Slaski's room.

I wasn't lying, either. It *was* lunchtime. The fact that we weren't technically supposed to leave school grounds at lunch? Well, I didn't feel that was important to mention. I was less worried about facing the wrath of Sister Ernestine when she found out I was skipping school than I was about explaining to my stepbrother Brad why I'd so desperately needed the keys to the Land Rover. Just because Brad had happened to get his driver's license about five seconds before I'd gotten mine (well, okay, a few weeks before I'd gotten mine, actually), he seems to feel that the ancient Land Rover, which is supposed to be the "kids' car," belongs solely to him, and that only he's allowed to ferry the two of us, plus his little brother, David, to and from school every day.

I'd had to resort to using the words "feminine hygiene products" and "glove compartment" just to get him to surrender the keys. I had no idea what he was going to do when I didn't return before the end of lunch and he discovered the car was gone. Narc on me, doubtlessly. It seemed to be his one joy in life.

Sadly, I never seem able to return the favor, thanks to Brad generally having some kind of goods on me.

In any case, I wasn't going to squander what precious little time I had wondering what Brad was going to say about my taking the car. Instead, I hurried into Paul's grandfather's bedroom.

As usual, the Game Show Network was on. The attendant had parked Dr. Slaski's wheelchair in front of the plasma screen television. Dr. Slaski himself, however, appeared to be paying no attention whatsoever to Bob Barker. Instead, he was staring fixedly at a spot in the center of the highly polished tile floor.

I wasn't fooled by this, however.

"Dr. Slaski?" I picked up the remote and turned the TV volume down, then hurried to the doctor's side. "Dr. Slaski, it's me, Suze. Paul's friend, Suze? I need to talk to you for a minute."

Paul's grandfather didn't respond. Unless you call drooling a response.

"Dr. Slaski," I said, pulling up a chair so that I could sit closer to his ear. I didn't want the attendant to overhear our discussion, so I was trying to keep my voice low. "Dr. Slaski, your nurse isn't here and neither is Paul. It's just the two of us. I need to talk to you about something Paul's been telling me. About, er, mediators. It's important."

As soon as he heard that neither Paul nor his attendant was nearby, a change seemed to come over Dr. Slaski. He straightened up in his chair, lifting his head so he could fix me with a rheumy-eyed stare. The drooling stopped right away.

"Oh," he said when he saw it was me. He didn't exactly look thrilled. "You again."

I didn't think that was completely fair, seeing as how the last time the two of us had spoken, *he* had sought *me* out . . . sought me out to deliver a cryptic warning about his own grandson, whom he'd equated to the devil, no less.

But I decided to let that slide.

"Yes, it's me, Dr. Slaski," I said. "Suze. Listen. About Paul."

"What's that little pisser been up to now?"

Clearly there is very little love lost between Dr. Slaski and his grandson.

"Nothing," I said. "Yet. At least, so far as I can tell. It's what he says he can do."

"What's that, then?" Dr. Slaski asked. "And this better be good. *Family Feud* comes on in five minutes."

Good God. Was I, I wondered, going to end up wheelchair bound and addicted to game shows when I was Dr. Slaski's age? Because Dr. Slaski—or Mr. Slater, as Paul wanted everyone to think of him—is also a mediator, one who'd gone to the ends of the earth looking to find answers about his unusual talent. Apparently, he'd found what he was looking for in the tombs of ancient Egypt.

Problem is, nobody believed him. Not about the existence of a race of people whose sole duty it was to guide the spirits of the dead to their ultimate destinations, and certainly not that he, Dr. Slaski, was one of them. The old man's many writings on the subject, most of them self-published, went ignored by the scientific and academic communities, and were now gathering dust in plastic bins beneath his grandson's bed.

Worse, Dr. Slaski's own family seem to be trying to sweep *him* under the bed, as well, Paul's father even having gone so far as to change his name to avoid being associated with the old man.

And what had Dr. Slaski gotten for all his efforts? A terminal illness and his grandson, Paul, for company. The illness, or so Dr. Slaski claimed, had been brought on by spending too much time in the "shadowland"—that way station between this world and the next. And Paul?

Well, he had brought Paul on all by himself.

I guess he had a reason to feel bitterly toward the human race. But why he felt that way toward Paul, I was only just learning.

I tried to start out slowly, so he'd be sure to understand.

"Paul says mediators—"

"Shifters." Dr. Slaski insisted people like him and Paul and me are more properly called shifters, for our (in my case, newly discovered) ability to shift between the dimensions of the living and the dead. "Shifters, girl, I told you before. Don't make me say it again."

"Shifters," I corrected myself. "Paul says that shifters have the ability to time travel."

"Indeed," Dr. Slaski said. "What of it?"

I gaped at him. I couldn't help it. If he'd hit me in the back of the head with a piñata stick, I could not have been more surprised. "You . . . you *knew* about this?"

"Of course I know about it," Dr. Slaski said acidly. "Who do you think wrote the paper that gave that fool grandson of mine the idea?"

This is what I got for not paying more attention during my mediator sessions with Paul.

"But why didn't you *tell* me?"

Dr. Slaski looked at me very sarcastically. "You didn't ask," he said.

I sat there like a lump staring at him. I couldn't believe it. All this time . . . all this time I'd had *another* skill I'd known nothing about. But what would I have ever needed the ability to time travel for, anyway? I guess there were a few bad hair days I wouldn't have minded going back and fixing, but other than that . . .

Then, like a bolt of lightning, it hit me.

My dad. I could go back through time and save my dad.

No. No, it didn't work that way. It couldn't. Because if it could . . . if it could . . .

Then everything would be different.

Everything.

Dr. Slaski coughed, hard. I shook myself and touched his shoulder.

"Dr. Slaski? Are you all right?"

"What do you think?" Dr. Slaski demanded, not very graciously. "I've got six months to live. Maybe less, if those damned doctors have their way and keep bleeding the life out of me. You think I'm all right?"

"I . . ." It was selfish of me, I knew, but I didn't have time to listen to his health problems. I needed to know more about this new power he—and possibly I—had.

"How?" I demanded eagerly. "How do you do it? Travel through time, I mean."

Dr. Slaski glanced at the TV. Fortunately the credits for *The Price Is Right* were still rolling. *Family Feud* hadn't started yet.

"It's easy," he said. "If my idiot grandson can figure it out, any moron can."

We didn't have much time. *Family Feud* was going to start at any second.

"How?" I asked him again. "*How?*"

"You need something," the doctor said with exaggerated patience, like he was talking to a five-year-old. "Something of the time you want to go to. To anchor you to it."

I thought of a time-travel movie I had seen. "Like a coin?" I asked.

"A coin would do it," Dr. Slaski said, though he looked skeptical. "Of course, you'd need to use a coin that had once been owned by a specific person who existed in the time you want to go to, and who'd once actually stood where you're standing. And you need to pick a spot you can get back to without shifting onto some innocent bystander."

"You mean—" I blinked. "You mean when you go back, *all* of you goes back? Not just—"

"Your soul?" Dr. Slaski snorted. "Lot of good that what do, wandering around in some other century without any body. No, when you go, you *go*. That's why you've got to be smart about it. You can't just go hopping through time and space all willy-nilly, you know. Not if you want to keep your guts from spilling out. You've got to go to a spot where you knew the person once stood, hold the object they once owned, and—"

"And?" I asked breathlessly.

"Close your eyes and shift." Dr. Slaski looked back at the television, bored by the whole conversation.

"And that's it?" It *was* easy. "You mean I can just pop back through time and visit anyone I want?"

"Of course not," Dr. Slaski said, his gaze glued to the TV screen. It was almost as an afterthought that he added, "He's got to be dead, of course. And someone you've mediated. I never determined why, but it must have something to do with that person's energy, or being. Must be the link . . ." Dr. Slaski trailed off, lost in research done decades before.

"You mean . . ." I blinked in confusion. "We can only go back through time if it's to help a ghost?"

"Give the girl a prize," Dr. Slaski drawled, turning his gaze back toward the television.

For once I didn't mind his sarcasm. Because ghosts? Ghosts I can deal with. Ghosts like . . .

. . . well, my dad, for instance.

And I had plenty of stuff that once belonged to Dad. I still had the shirt he'd been wearing the day he died. I had plucked it from the pile of things the hospital had given us and kept it under my pillow for months after he'd died . . . right up until the day I finally saw him again, when he appeared to me, and told me exactly why it was that I, but not Mom, could see him.

I thought my mom hadn't known about it—the shirt, I mean—but now I knew she must have. She surely would have found it when she was making my bed or playing tooth fairy.

But she had never said anything. To be fair, she *couldn't* say anything, because she kept Dad's ashes in his favorite beer stein for years before we finally got the guts to scatter them in the park where he'd died, the park he'd loved so much, just before her wedding to Andy.

A park, I realized, I'd have to go to if I wanted to go back through time to save him, because the apartment we'd lived in had been sold and I couldn't very well walk up to the new owners and be all "Can I stand in your living room for a minute? I just need to pop back through time to save my dad's life."

Of course, both the park and the apartment were all the way across the country. But I had some babysitting money saved up. Maybe even enough for a plane ticket . . .

I could do it. I could totally keep my dad from dying.

"What else?" I asked Dr. Slaski, with a glance at the TV. A commercial, thank God. "When you have the . . . thing that belonged to the ghost, and you're standing in a spot where he once stood? What do you do then?"

Dr. Slaski looked annoyed. "You hold the object—that's your anchor—and nothing else. That's important, you know. You can't be touching anything else or you could end up taking it with you. Then you picture the person. And then you go. Easy as pie." Dr. Slaski nodded at the TV. "Turn it up. *Feud*'ll be on in a minute."

I couldn't believe it was so easy. Just like that, I could go back through time and keep someone I loved from dying.

"Of course," Dr. Slaski said casually, "once you get there—to where you're going—you have to watch yourself. You don't want to be changing history . . . at least, not too much. You have to weigh the consequences of your actions very carefully."

I didn't say anything. What possible consequences could my saving my dad have? Except that my mom, instead of crying into her pillow every night for years after he died—right up until she met Andy, actually—would be happy? That *I* would be happy?

Then it hit me. Andy. If my dad had lived, my mother would never have met Andy. Or rather, she might have met him, but she would never have married him.

And then we would never have moved to California.

And I would never have met Jesse.

Suddenly, the full impact of what Dr. Slaski had said sunk in. "Oh," I said.

His gaze—despite the glaucoma that clouded his blue eyes, which otherwise were like a photocopy of Paul's—was sharp.

"I thought there'd be an *oh* in there somewhere," he said. "Not as easy as you thought, shifting through time, is it? And keep in mind the fact that the longer you stay in a time not your own, the longer your recovery time when you do get back to the present," Dr. Slaski added not very pleasantly.

"Recovery time? You mean like . . . it gives you a headache?" Which was what shifting gave me. Every time.

Dr. Slaski looked amused about something. His gaze wasn't on the television screen, so I knew it was something to do with what I'd just said.

"Little worse than a headache," he said dryly, and patted the mattress beneath him. "Unless you mean that as a euphemism for losing a host of brain cells. And that's the least of what could happen to you. Time shift too many times and you'll be a vegetable before you're old enough to buy beer, I can guarantee."

"Does Paul know that?" I asked. "I mean, about the . . . losing brain cells thing?"

"He should," Dr. Slaski said, "if he read my paper on it."

And yet he still wanted to try it.

"Why would Paul want to go back through time?" I asked. He could hardly be motivated by a desire to help anyone, as the only person Paul Slater had ever been interested in helping was . . . well, Paul Slater.

"How should I know?" Dr. Slaski looked bored. "I don't understand why you spend any time at all with that boy. I told you he was no good. Just like his father, that one is, ashamed of me. . . ."

I didn't pay attention to Dr. Slaski's diatribe against his grandson. I was too busy thinking. What was it Paul had said the other night, in the Gutierrezes' backyard? That he wouldn't kill Jesse . . .

. . . but that he might do something to keep Jesse from having died in the first place.

That was when it finally dawned on me. Standing there in Dr. Slaski's bedroom, while he fumbled for the remote, found the volume button, and cried, "Damnit, we missed the first category!"

Paul was going back through time. To Jesse's time.

And not to kill him.

To save his life.

chapter *seven*

"Father Dominic?" My voice seemed frantic, even to my own ears. "Father D., are you there?"

"Yes, Susannah." Father Dominic sounded frazzled. But then, that could be because he still hadn't figured out how to work his cell phone. "Yes, I'm here. I thought you had to hit the Send button to answer, but apparently—"

"Father Dominic, something terrible has happened." I didn't wait for him to respond, but just plunged ahead. "Paul's figured out a way to go back through time, and he's going to go back to the day Jesse died and save his life."

There was a long pause. Then Father Dominic said, "Susannah. Where are you?"

I looked around. I was standing in Paul's kitchen, using the wall-mounted phone I had found there. I'd asked Dr. Slaski's attendant after I'd left his patient, if I could use the phone. He'd told me to go right ahead.

"I'm at Paul's house," I said. "Father Dominic, did you

hear me? Paul's figured out a way to keep Jesse from dying."

"Well," Father Dominic said, "That's wonderful news. But shouldn't you be in school? It's only just a little past one o'clock—"

"Father D.!" I practically screamed. "You don't understand! If Paul keeps Jesse from dying, *then Jesse and I will never meet!*"

"Hmmm." Father Dominic took his sweet time to consider what I'd said. "Altering the course of history is never a good idea, I suppose. Look what happened in that film. What was it? Oh, yes. *Back to the Future.*"

"*Father Dominic.*" I was practically crying with frustration. "Please, this isn't a movie. It's my *life.* You've got to help me. You've got to come back here and help me stop him. He won't listen to me. I know he won't. But he might listen to you. . . ."

"Well, I couldn't possibly come back now, Susannah," Father Dominic said. "The monsignor isn't—well, the, er, hot dog appeared to be lodged in his throat for longer than anyone thought . . . Susannah, did you say Paul's figured out a way to *travel through time?*"

"Yes," I said from between gritted teeth. I was beginning to regret having kept Father Dominic in the dark about so much of what I'd learned from Paul during our Wednesday afternoons together.

"Goodness," Father Dominic said. "How interesting. And how do you suppose he does that?"

"All he needs is something old," I said. "Something

belonging to the person, you know, he wants to travel back to see. The person has to be a ghost, a ghost that he's met. And then he just has to stand in a place he knows that person will be—in his head, you know—and he's there."

"Good heavens," Father Dominic said. "Do you know what this means, Susannah?"

"Yes," I said miserably. "It means that I'm going to move to Carmel, and there isn't going to be anybody haunting my bedroom because Jesse will never have been killed there."

"No," Father Dominic said. "Well, I mean, yes, I suppose it does mean that. But more important, it means we could prevent the deaths of all of the ghosts we encounter, just by popping back through time and—"

"We can't," I interrupted flatly. "Unless we want to end up with six months left to live, like Paul's grandfather. It isn't like shifting to the spirit plane. Your whole body goes . . . and, I guess, suffers the consequences. But Paul's just planning the one trip."

"Yes," Father Dominic said, sounding distant—more distant than San Francisco, anyway. "Yes, I see."

"Father Dominic!" I cried. I was losing him . . . and not just because our phone connection wasn't the best. "You've got to stop him!"

"But why should I, Susannah?" Father Dominic asked. "What Paul plans on doing is quite generous, actually."

"*Generous*?" I cried. "What's so *generous* about it?"

"He's giving Jesse another chance at life," Father Dominic said. "And, from what you say, risking his own life in the process. I'd say it's quite noble of him, actually."

"Noble!" I couldn't believe my ears. "Father Dom, I can assure you, Paul's motives are far from noble. He's only doing it . . ."

"Yes?" Father Dominic was suddenly all ears.

But how can you explain to a priest that a guy is trying to off your boyfriend so he can get into your pants?

Especially when Paul wasn't trying to off Jesse at all, but to save his life, actually? "It's just . . ." I wasn't making any sense, but I didn't care. "Can't you expel him or something?"

"No, Susannah," Father Dominic said. Was it my imagination or was there a slight chuckle in his voice? "I can't expel him. Not for that, anyway."

"But we have to stop him," I said. My protests, even to my own ears, were starting to grow faint. "It's . . . it's *unnatural*, what he's planning on doing."

"That may very well be," Father Dominic said, "but it isn't immoral. It isn't even illegal, as far as I can tell."

This had to be a first. Paul doing something that could actually be construed as moral, I mean.

"—But I do wonder," Father Dominic went on thoughtfully, "just how he's planning on accomplishing this little miracle."

"I told you," I said bitterly. "All he has to do is get something the person once owned, and then stand in a place he once stood, and—"

"Yes," Father Dominic said. "But what belonging of Jesse's does Paul have?"

This shut me up for a minute. Because Father Dominic was right. Paul didn't have anything of Jesse's. He couldn't stop Jesse's murder, because he didn't own anything from Jesse's past.

"Oh," I said, beginning to feel a little less like I had a slowly tightening noose around my neck. "Oh. You're right."

"Of course I am," Father Dominic said. Was it my imagination or did he sound distracted? "Although it's something you might think of doing, Susannah. If he'll teach you how, I mean."

"What?" I twisted the phone cord around my finger. "Go back through time and save Jesse from dying?"

"Exactly," Father Dominic said. "It might, for all you know, be the reason why he's still here on earth. Because he was never meant to die in the first place."

I was so appalled that for a moment, I couldn't say anything. Unbidden, my mind flashed back to that poster my ninth grade English teacher had hung up in her classroom, of two seagulls flying over a beach. . . . A poster I always seemed to remember at the most inconvenient moments. IF YOU LOVE SOMETHING, LET IT GO, the words beneath the seagulls read. IF IT WAS MEANT TO BE, IT WILL COME BACK TO YOU.

The imaginary noose around my neck tightened to a choking point.

"That's bull, Father D.," I yelled into the phone. "Do you hear me? *Bull!*"

"Susannah—" Father Dominic sounded startled.

"That is NOT why Jesse is still here," I shouted. "It's

NOT. Jesse and I are meant to be together, and if you can't see that, well, that's your own damn problem!"

Now Father Dominic sounded more than startled. He sounded angry. "Susannah," he said. "There's no reason to use that kind of language—"

"No, there's not," I agreed with him. "Especially since I have nothing more to say to you." I slammed the phone back down into its cradle. A second later, Dr. Slaski's attendant appeared, looking worried.

"Susan?" he asked. "You all right?"

"I'm fine," I said, horrified to find that my cheeks were damp.

Great. So, on top of everything else, I'd been crying.

"It's just," the attendant said, "I heard shouting. . . ."

"It's nothing," I said. "I'm leaving. Don't worry."

And I did, without saying good-bye to Dr. Slaski. I had no more to say to him than I did to Father Dom. There was only one person, I realized, who could stop Paul from doing what I now knew he was going to do.

And that person was me.

Of course, knowing that fact wasn't the same as actually having a plan for how I was going to stop him. That's what I tried to come up with as I drove back to school. A plan.

It wasn't until I was pulling into the Mission Academy's student parking lot that what Father Dominic had said really began to sink in. Paul didn't have anything of Jesse's that could bring him back to that horrible night when Jesse had died. I was almost sure of it. Jesse had been murdered and his body never found—until recently, that is. His own family had believed he'd run away to escape an unwanted marriage.

What could Paul possibly have of Jesse's that could help him get back to the day leading up to his death? Nothing. Because the only things that still existed from that time were a miniature portrait of Jesse—which I kept safe at home—and some letters he'd written to his fiancée. But those were on display at the Carmel Historical Society museum.

There was nothing of Jesse's that Paul could possibly have that he could use to hurt him. Or rather, to save him. Nothing. Jesse was safe.

Which meant that *I* was safe.

The relief I felt was short-lived, however. Oh, not my relief about Jesse. That remained. It was as I was attempting to sneak back into school that my newly restored equilibrium was shaken again. Only this time, it wasn't by Paul. No, it was Sister Ernestine who shattered my hard-won sense of calm, just as I was trying to blend in with my fellow students as they made their way to their next class, pretending like I'd been there with them all along.

"Susannah Simon!" The vice principal's shrill voice caused several doves that had been roosting in the beams overhead to take off in startled flight. "Come to my office immediately!"

My youngest stepbrother, David, happened to be nearby. When he heard the sister's command, he visibly paled . . . an accomplishment for him, seeing how pale he was already, being a redhead.

"Suze," he asked me, looking a bit freaked. And why not? Usually when I get into trouble, it isn't for mere tardiness. No, more often, it's along the lines of destruction of property . . . and someone usually ends up unconscious, if not dead. "What did you do *now*?"

"Never mind," I said, a little chagrined that I'd been busted for so minor an offense as skipping class. I was really losing my touch.

I followed Sister Ernestine into her office, which, unlike Father Dominic's, didn't have any teaching awards on the shelves. No one would consider Sister Ernestine an exemplary educator. She's a disciplinarian, plain and simple.

I got off lightly, I suppose. She'd noticed I'd been gone during religion class, which I was supposed to have right after lunch. I told her I'd had a slight medical emergency, and needed to go to the drugstore, once again invoking the 'crimson tide' in the hope she'd drop the subject. It didn't have the same effect on Sister Ernestine as it had on Brad, however.

"Then you should have gone to the nurse's office," was Sister Ernestine's terse response.

For my crime, I was assigned to write a thousand-word essay on the importance of honoring one's commitments. Additionally, I was told to be at Saturday's antique auction to help man the eighth graders' bake sale table.

All in all, I suppose it could have been worse.

Or so I thought. Before I ran into Paul Slater.

He was lurking behind one of the stone supports that hold up the breezeway, which is why I didn't spot him on my way from Sister Ernestine's office to my trig class. He stepped out from the shadows just as I was hurrying by.

"The wanderer returneth," he said.

I flattened a hand to my chest, as if doing so would cause my heart, which had practically jumped through my ribs at the sight of him, to beat normally again.

"Why do you have to do that?" I demanded testily. "You scared the pants off me."

"I wish." Paul's smile was decidedly irreligious, considering the fact that we were standing only a few hundred feet away from a church. "So. Where'd you disappear to?"

I could have lied, I suppose. But what would have been the point? He'd learn the truth as soon as he got home and his grandfather's attendant told him I'd stopped by.

So I stuck out my chin and, ignoring my stuttering pulse, plunged. "Your place," I said.

Paul's dark eyebrows came down in a rush as he frowned. "*My* place? What'd you go to *my* place for?"

"To have a chat," I barreled on, "with your grandfather."

Paul's scowl grew even deeper. "My grandfather?" He shook his head. "What the hell would you want to go see him for? The guy's a complete gork."

"He's not well," I agreed. "But he's still capable of carrying on a conversation."

"Yeah," Paul said with a sneer. "About Richard Dawson, maybe."

"Well, that," I said, knowing what I was about to say next would enrage him, but also knowing that really, I didn't have any other choice, "and time travel."

Paul's eyes widened. As I'd expected, I'd shocked him.

"Time travel? You talked about *time travel*? With Grandpa Gork?"

"With Dr. Slaski," I corrected him. "And yes, I did."

The two words—doctor and Slaski—seemed to hit him like physical blows. He certainly looked as stunned as if I'd hit him.

"Are you . . ." He couldn't seem to find the right words to express himself. "Are you crazy?" is what he seemed to settle for.

"No," I said. "And neither is your grandfather. But I think *you* might be," I went on—recklessly, I knew, but no longer caring. Not now that I knew what he was after.

"I know your grandfather is Oliver Slaski," I stated. "He told me so himself."

He just stared at me. It was as if, right before his eyes, I was turning into a completely different person than the Suze he'd known. And maybe I was. I was certainly angrier at him than I'd ever been before—more than the first time, even, that he'd tried to get rid of Jesse. Because he hadn't known then what he surely knew by now. . . . That Paul and me?

Yeah, that was *never* going to happen.

"He didn't talk to you," Paul said finally, his blue eyes flat and cold as the Pacific in November. "He doesn't talk to anybody."

"Not to you, maybe," I said. "Why should he, when you treat him the way you do . . . like he's a big inconvenience, a—what do you call him?—Oh, yeah. A gork. I mean, your own father changed his name, he was so ashamed of him. But if you'd ever taken the time to find out, you'd know Dr. Slaski isn't as far gone as you think . . . and he has some pretty interesting things to say about you."

"I'm sure," Paul said with a smirk. "In fact, I'm pretty sure I can guess. I'm the spawn of Satan. I'm up to no good. And you should stay away from me. That about sum it up?"

"Pretty much," I said. "And considering that you plan on traveling back through time and keeping Jesse from dying? I'd say he's one hundred percent right."

At that, the flatness left his eyes—but not the coldness. He even smiled a little, though it was with just half his mouth. "So you finally figured it out, huh? Took you long enough—"

But I didn't let him finish. I took a step forward until my face was just inches below his, and said as fiercely as I could, "Well, I've figured it out now. And all I can say is that if you think making it so Jesse and I never met will change my feelings about you, you're dreaming."

Paul looked hurt. But I knew it was all just a put-on. Because Paul doesn't have feelings. Not if he really intends to do what I suspect.

But he was doing his best to prove me wrong.

"But, Suze," he said, his blue eyes wide and innocent. "I'm just doing what you want. After that whole thing with Mrs. Gutierrez, you got me thinking. . . . I'm really trying to tread the path of righteousness. And isn't saving Jesse's life the right thing to do? I mean, if you really love him, you must want what's best for him, don't you? And wouldn't his

85

living a long and happy life be what's best for him?"

I blinked at him, completely thrown by the way he'd twisted everything around.

"That isn't—I—" I couldn't seem to get the words out. All I could do was stand there and stammer.

"That's okay, Suze," Paul said, reaching up and laying a hand on my arm—to comfort me, I suppose, in my hour of need. "You don't have to thank me. Now, don't you think we'd better get back? You don't want Sister Ernestine to find you skipping class again, now, do you?"

I stared at him, dumbfounded. I had never in my life met anyone as manipulative as he was . . . with the exception, maybe, of my stepbrother Brad. Only Brad didn't have Paul's smarts and was rarely able to pull off anything more twisted than a house party . . . and even that had gotten busted by the cops.

"You're—you're high," I finally managed to stammer, "if you think saving Jesse that night—the night he died—will guarantee him a long life. Who's to say Diego won't try again the next night? Or the next? What are you going to do, stay in 1850 and become Jesse's personal bodyguard?"

"If that's what it takes," Paul said in a sickeningly sweet voice. "You see, I'd do anything—anything it takes—to make sure Jesse dies peacefully in his sleep at a ripe old age, so that he never, ever has need of a mediator."

The colors in the courtyard—the red roof tiles along the Mission, the pink hibiscus blossoms, the deep green of the palm fronds—spun dizzyingly around me as his words sunk in. I tasted something awful rising in my throat.

"Why are you doing this?" I stared up at him in horror. "You must know it will never work. Getting rid of Jesse won't make me care about you. *I don't like you in that way.*"

"Don't you?" Paul asked with a smile that was as cold as his gaze. "Funny, I could have sworn, the last time we kissed, that you did. At least a little. Enough, anyway—"

His voice trailed off suggestively . . . but just what he was suggesting, I couldn't imagine.

"Enough for what?" I demanded.

"Enough," Paul said, "that you're thinking about transferring my soul out of my body and throwing Jesse's in here instead."

chapter *eight*

"Don't bother denying it," Paul said as I stared up at him in utter shock. "I know that's what you've been planning ever since I first made the mistake of telling you about it." The heat from the hand he'd placed on my arm seemed to singe my skin. "My saving Jesse's life is more a preemptive strike than anything else. Because the truth is, I kind of like my body. I don't really want to give it up for him."

My mouth was moving—I know it was, because Paul seemed to be waiting for some kind of reply.

Only I couldn't make a sound. I was *that* stunned.

Because it finally made sense, now. That accusation Paul had hurled at me the other day in his kitchen. That his plans for Jesse were a lot more humane than what I'd had planned for Paul. Because he was planning on saving Jesse, whereas I, apparently, am planning on killing Paul.

Except, of course, that I'm not.

But that didn't seem to matter to him.

"It's okay," Paul assured me. "I mean, it's kind of flattering in a way, really. That you think I'm hot enough to put your boyfriend's soul into. It proves that, whatever you say, you do like me, a little. Or at least that you like making out with me."

"That is so"—I found my voice at last. Unfortunately, it came out shrill as a banshee's. I didn't care, though. All I cared about was proving to him how very, very wrong he was—"so untrue! How could you even—what could have given you the idea that I—"

"Oh, come on, Suze," Paul said. "Admit it. With me, it's the real thing. Don't tell me that when you're with Jesse, you aren't thinking about the fact that, cozy as things might get between the two of you, it's all an illusion. That isn't *really* his heart you hear beating in his chest. His skin isn't *really* warm. Because he doesn't *have* skin. It's all in your head. . . . Not like this," he added, gently stroking my arm with his thumb.

Until I wrenched my arm away, that is, and fell back a step. He looked taken aback, but held up both hands to indicate he wouldn't touch me again. "Whoa, okay, Suze. Sorry. But you can't deny it's true that, when we kiss, you don't exactly fight me off. At least, not right away—"

I felt my cheeks flame. I was so embarrassed. I couldn't believe he was bringing this up here, at *school*, of all places. . . .

. . . especially considering that Jesse? Yeah, this was his new stomping ground. He was undoubtedly around somewhere nearby.

But I couldn't deny what Paul was saying. I mean, I could, but I'd be lying.

"Of course I like it when you kiss me," I said, though I practically had to cough out every word, they stuck in my throat so badly. "You're a good kisser and you know it." What else could I say? It was true. "But that doesn't mean I like *you*."

Which was also true.

But it didn't seem to bother Paul.

"Proving my point," he said smugly, "that you want my body, but with Jesse's soul in it."

"I think what happened to Jesse was horrible," I said slowly, referring to the murder. "And okay, there pretty much isn't anything I wouldn't do if I thought it would bring him back to life. *But not that.*"

"Why not?" Paul asked with a shrug. "I mean, what's stopping you? As you've pointed out numerous times, I'm a reprehensible human being with no redeeming qualities . . . except for my kissing abilities, apparently. So why not just give my soul a yank and let the all-perfect Jesse have a second chance at life?"

The truth was, I really was innocent of what he was accusing me. It had never once occurred to me to do what he was insisting I'd been plotting for some time to do. Oh, okay, maybe I'd considered it in passing every now and then. But I'd always instantly dismissed the idea.

But now—perhaps because he was goading me into it— a part of me actually seemed to perk up and go *Why not?* Paul *didn't* deserve all the great things he had. He didn't even appreciate them! He stole from people less fortunate than he was, he didn't treat his family with anything like respect, and he certainly hadn't been very nice to me . . . or to Jesse.

Why *couldn't* I send Paul off to the great unknown, and let Jesse have Paul's body . . . and his life? Jesse deserved a second chance, and he'd certainly be a better Paul Slater than Paul had ever been. . . .

Of course, Jesse wouldn't like it. He would definitely think it was wrong to rob Paul of the life that was rightfully his, just so he could have a chance to live again.

And it *would* be weird, looking into Paul's blue eyes and knowing Jesse was looking out of them.

But it wouldn't *really* be like I was killing Paul. His body would still be alive. And his soul would be . . . well, right where Jesse's was now, aimlessly wandering the earth, with no idea what was going to happen to him next.

But then sanity returned, cold and dampening as the water burbling in the fountain in the center of the Mission's courtyard. And I heard myself answering Paul's question— *So why not just give my soul a yank and let the all-perfect Jesse have a second chance at life?*—every bit as coolly as he'd asked it.

"Um," I said sarcastically, "because that would be *murder*, maybe?"

Some muscles in Paul's jaw tightened. "Justifiable homicide at best," he said. "And we both know I wouldn't really be dead. And I would deserve it, wouldn't I? For my sins?"

"Maybe so," I said, feeling the way I usually did after long session with my kickboxing exercise video. You know, the endorphins rushing in. Because I really had, in a way, just had a major workout. This one just happened to be an emotional one. "But the fact is, I'm not the one to judge."

"Why not?" Paul asked. "You don't seem to have a problem when it comes to judging *me.*"

But he wasn't going to get me with that one. "Your grandfather warned me once that when he'd realized all the things we mediators could do, he'd made the mistake of thinking he was God," I told him. "And look where that got him. I won't be making the same mistake."

Paul just blinked at me. I really think he'd believed I'd meant to do it. The soul transference thing, I mean. Now that I'd taken all the wind out of his sails, he seemed . . . well, as stunned as I'd been earlier.

"So you see," I said while I still had the advantage, "your whole going-back-through-time-to-save-Jesse scheme? It's kind of pointless. Because for one thing, you can't travel back through time unless the person you're going back to see actually wants your help . . . which Jesse most definitely does not. And, for another, I was never going to steal your body and give it to Jesse, Paul. But, you know, you can keep on flattering yourself that I was, if it makes you happy."

I shouldn't, I realized a moment too late, have been quite so flippant. At least not then. Because when I attempted to stroll by him after that last remark—even giving my hair a toss to show my disdain for him—something inside him seemed to snap. Next thing I knew, his hand had shot out and caught my arm in a grip that hurt.

"Oh no, you don't," he snarled. "You're not getting away that easily—"

But he was wrong. Because the very next second, Paul's hand had been pried off me and his arm was bent behind his back in what looked to be a pretty painful position.

"Hasn't anyone ever told you," Jesse asked, in a semi-amused voice, "that a gentleman never lays a hand on a lady?"

Which I thought was kind of funny, considering where Jesse had had *his* hand the last time I'd seen him. But I thought it better to let that slide.

"Jesse," I said. "I'm okay. You can let him go."

But Jesse didn't loosen his grip. If anyone had happened to walk by, they'd have seen Paul bent over at a peculiar angle, his face white with pain. Because of course, only he and I could see the ghost who had hold of him.

"I wasn't gonna do anything to her," Paul insisted in a strangled voice. "I swear!"

Jesse looked at me for confirmation of this.

"Did he hurt you, Susannah?" he asked.

I shook my head. "I'm all right," I said.

Jesse held on to Paul for a second or two longer—just, I think, to prove he could—then he let go, so suddenly that Paul lost his balance and fell to his hands and knees, onto the stone slabs that made up the floor of the breezeway.

"You didn't have to call *him*," Paul said to me, with wounded dignity.

"I didn't." I was telling the truth, too.

"She didn't have to," Jesse said, going to lean against one of the breezeway's support pillars. He folded his arms across his chest and looked at Paul dispassionately as he climbed to his feet and brushed himself off.

"What'd you, sense a disturbance in the Force, or something?" Paul asked testily.

"Something like that." Jesse looked from Paul to me and then back again. "Is there anything going on here that I should know about?"

"No," I said quickly. Too quickly, maybe, since one of Jesse's eyebrows—the one with the scar through it—went up inquisitively.

Paul, to my fury, burst out into scornful laughing.

"Oh yeah," he said. "You two have a *great* relationship. It's really great how *honest* you are with each other."

Jesse narrowed his dark eyes in Paul's direction. That seemed to cause some of his laughter to dry up, without Jesse even having to say a word.

Then Jesse turned his penetrating gaze on me.

"It's nothing," I blurted, feeling a little panicky all of a sudden. "Paul was just . . . he was thinking of doing something to you. But he changed his mind. Didn't you, Paul?"

"Not really," Paul said. "Hey, I have an idea. Let's ask *Jesse* what he'd want, shall we? Say, Jesse, how would feel if I told you I could—"

"No," I interrupted with a gasp. Suddenly, it was getting very difficult to breathe. "Paul, really, that's not necessary. Jesse won't—"

"Now, Suze," Paul said as if he were speaking to a three-year-old. "Let's allow Jesse to decide. Jesse, what if I told you that in addition to all the many other wonderful things that we mediators can do, it turned out we can also travel through time? And that I had generously offered to travel back to your time—the night you died, I mean—and save your life. What would you say to that?"

Jesse's dark gaze didn't leave Paul's face, nor did his expression waver from cold disdain. Not even for a second.

"I would say that you're a liar" was Jesse's preternaturally calm response.

"See, I thought you might say that." Paul had the smooth patter and the self-confidence of a traveling salesman giving his spiel. "But I'm here to tell you it's the absolute truth. Think about it, Jesse. You didn't have to die that night. I can go back through time and warn you. Well, you won't know me, of course, but I think if I tell you—the past you—that I'm from the future and that you're going to die if you don't do what I tell you, you'll believe me."

"Do you?" Jesse asked in the same deadly calm voice. "Because I don't."

That stumped Paul for a second or two, during which my breathing became easy again. My heart swelled with affection for the man leaning against the stone pillar beside me. I shouldn't have worried about hiding this from Jesse. Jesse would never choose life over me. Never. He loves me too much.

Or so I thought, before Paul started his patter once again.

"I don't think you understand what I'm saying here." Paul shook his head. "I'm talking about giving you back your *life*, Jesse. None of this wandering around in a sort of half-life for a hundred and fifty years, watching the people you love grow older and die, one by one. No way. You'll *live*. To a ripe old age, if I can, you know, get rid of that Diego guy who killed you. I mean, how can you say no to an offer like that?"

"Like this," Jesse said tonelessly. "No."

Yes! I thought, flushing with joy. *Yes!*

Paul blinked. Once. Twice.

Then he said, his voice devoid of the friendliness that had been in it moments before, "Don't be an idiot. I'm offering you a chance to live again. *Live*. What are you going to do, hang around here for the rest of eternity? Are you going to watch *her* get old"—he thrust a finger at me—"and eventually turn to dust like you did with your family? Don't you remember how that felt? You want to go through all that again? You want her to sacrifice having a normal life— marriage, kids, grandkids—just to be with you, when you can't even support her, can't even—"

"Paul, stop it," I commanded because I could see Jesse's face growing less and less expressionless with every word.

But Paul wasn't done. Not by a long shot.

"You think you're doing *her* any favors by sticking around?" he demanded. "Man, you're only keeping her from leading a normal life—"

"Stop it!" I shouted at Paul as I reached out and grasped Jesse by the arm.

Two things happened at once then. The first was that classroom doors suddenly flew open all around us and students began streaming out into the breezeway as they changed classes for the next period.

The next was that I seized Jesse's arms with both my hands and, looking up anxiously into his face, said, "Don't listen to him. Please. I don't care about those things, marriage and kids. All I want is you."

But it was too late. I could tell it was too late. Some of what Paul had said was already starting to sink in. Jesse's expression had grown troubled, and he seemed unable to look me in the eye.

"I mean it," I said, giving him a frustrated shake. "Don't pay attention to a word he says!"

"Um, hello, Suze." Kelly Prescott's voice rose above the noise of slamming lockers and chitchat. "Talk to the wall much?"

I flung a glance over my shoulder and saw her standing there with the rest of the Dolce and Gabbana Nazis, smirking at me. I knew, of course, what they were seeing. Me with hands raised, clutching nothing but air, and speaking to one of the pillars in the breezeway.

Like I don't have enough of a reputation for being a freak. Now I *really* looked like I was going around the bend.

But when I turned my head back to tell Jesse we'd finish this conversation later, I saw that I was too late. He'd already disappeared.

I dropped my hands and turned to face Paul, who still stood there looking angry and defensive and pleased with himself at the same time.

"Thanks a lot," I said to him.

"Don't mention it." He walked away, whistling to himself.

chapter *nine*

"Is there wheat in this?" a petite woman in a China chop and huge dark sunglasses asked me as she held up a chocolate chip cookie.

"Yes," I said.

"What about this?" She held up a brownie.

"Yes," I said.

"What about this?" A Mexican wedding cookie.

"Yes."

"Are you telling me," she demanded, looking outraged, "that there is wheat in *all* of these baked goods?"

I lowered my chair. I'd been tilting it out of boredom, to see how far back I could lean without falling.

"Because Tyler doesn't eat wheat," the woman went on, her hand going to cradle the chubby-cheeked face of a kid standing beside her. His blue eyes blinked out at me past his mother's perfectly manicured nails. "I'm raising him on a gluten-free diet."

"Try one of those," I said, pointing to some lemon bars.

"Is there dairy in it?" the woman asked suspiciously. "Because I'm raising Tyler lactose-free, as well."

"Dairy- and gluten-free, I promise," I said.

The woman slipped me a dollar, and I handed her the lemon bars. She passed one to Tyler, who inspected it, bit into it . . . then gave me a dazzling smile—his first of the day, no doubt—as his mother took his hand and led him away. Beside me, Shannon, my fellow bake sale attendant, looked appalled.

"There's wheat *and* dairy in those lemon bars," she said.

"I know." I rocked my chair back again. "I felt bad for the little guy."

"But—"

"She didn't say he was allergic. She just said she was raising him without it. Poor kid."

"Suu-uuze," the eighth grader said, giving my name multiple syllables. "You are so cool. Your brother Dave said you were cool, but I didn't believe him."

"Oh, I'm cool, all right," I assured her. It was weird to hear someone call David "Dave." He was such a David to me.

"You so are," Shannon said with perfect seriousness.

Whatever. It was so the story of my life to be stuck running a school bake sale while the rest of the world was enjoying such a perfect Saturday. The sky overhead was so blue and cloudless, it was almost painful to look at. The temperature was hovering at an extremely comfortable seventy degrees. A beautiful day for the beach or cappuccino at an outdoor café, or even just a walk.

And where was I? Yeah, that'd be manning the eighth grade bake sale booth at the Mission's charity antique auction.

"I couldn't believe it when Sister Ernestine told us *you* would be helping out at the booth," Shannon was saying. Shannon, I'd discovered, was not shy. She likes to talk. A lot. "I mean, you being an eleventh grader and all. And, you know. So cool."

Cool. Yeah, right.

I hadn't expected so many people to show up at the auction. Oh, sure, a few parents, eager to look like they cared about their kids' school. But not, you know, hordes of eager antique collectors.

But that's exactly who was here. There were people everywhere, people I'd never seen before, all wandering around, peering at the items that would be auctioned off, and whispering conspiratorially to one another. Occasionally, some of them stopped by our booth and shelled out a buck for a Rice Krispies treat or whatever. But mostly they had their eyes on the prize. . . . In this case, a hideously ugly wicker birdcage, or some old Mickey Mouse watch, or a snow globe of the Golden Gate Bridge, or some other equally non-designer thing.

The bidding got started late because the monsignor was supposed to have been acting as auctioneer. Because he was still in a coma up in San Francisco, there appeared to have been some frantic phone calls on the part of Sister Ernestine, as she looked for someone worthy to fill in.

You can imagine my surprise when she got up onto the dais at the end of the courtyard and announced into the microphone, in front of all the many antique collectors gathered there, that in the monsignor's absence, the auction would be called by none other than Andy Ackerman, well-known host of a home repair show on cable . . .

. . . and my stepdad.

I saw Andy climb the dais, waving modestly and looking abashed at all the applause he was getting. Not sure if there could possibly be anything more embarrassing than this, I started to slink down in my chair. . . .

Oh but wait, there *was* something more embarrassing than my stepfather calling the school antique auction. There was also the fact that most of the applause he was getting was coming from a woman in the front row.

My mother.

"Hey," Shannon said. "Isn't that—"

"Yes," I interrupted her. "Yes, it is."

A few minutes later the auction began, with Andy doing a very good imitation of those auctioneers you see on TV, the ones who talk really fast. He was gesturing to an ugly orange plastic chair and declaring it "authentic Eames" and asking if anyone would be willing to bid a hundred dollars for it.

A hundred dollars? I wouldn't have traded a Rice Krispies treat for it.

But wouldn't you know it, people in the audience were lifting their paddles, and soon the chair went for 350 bucks! And nobody even complained about what a rip-off it was.

Clearly Sister Ernestine had impressed upon this audience just how badly the school needed its basketball court repaved, because people were just throwing their money away on the most worthless pieces of garbage ever. I saw CeeCee's aunt Pru and my own homeroom teacher Mr. Walden both bidding against each other for an extremely hideous lamp. Aunt Pru finally won it—for 175 bucks—then walked over to Mr. Walden, apparently to gloat. Except that a few minutes later, I saw them having lemonade together and overheard them laughing about sharing custody of the lamp, like it was a kid in a divorce settlement. Shannon, observing this, went, "Aw, isn't that cute?"

Except that it totally wasn't. It totally isn't cute when your best friend's weird aunt and your homeroom teacher make a love connection, and you yourself can't get the guy you like to call you, because, oh guess what, he's a ghost and doesn't have a phone.

Not that if Jesse'd call, I'd have had anything much to say to him. What was I going to do, be all *"Oh, yeah, by the way, Paul wants to travel through time and make it so you never died. But I plan on stopping him. Because I want you to roam around in the netherworld for a hundred and fifty years so you and I can make out in my mom's car. Okay? Buh-bye."*

Besides, it wasn't like it was going to happen. Paul going back through time, I mean. Because he didn't have that anchor thing his grandpa had been talking about. The thing to anchor him to the night Jesse died.

Or that's what I was telling myself—reassuring myself—

103

right up until Andy held up the silver belt buckle Brad had found while he'd been cleaning out the attic. When he'd found it—wedged between the floorboards beneath the attic window—it had been this tarnished, crusty old thing I'd barely glanced at twice. Andy had thrown it into the box marked MISSION AUCTION, and I hadn't really thought about it again.

When he held it up now, I saw it winking in the afternoon sunlight. Someone had washed and polished it. And now Andy was going on about how it was an artifact from when our house had been the area's only hotel—a fancy way of saying what it had really been a boardinghouse— and that the Carmel Historical Society had put its age at close to 150 years.

About as long, actually, as my boyfriend had been dead.

"What'll I get for this sterling silver buckle?" Andy wanted to know. "A real piece of old-fashioned craftsmanship. Look at the detail in the ornate D carved into it."

Shannon, sitting beside me, suddenly went, "Does your brother ever talk about me? Dave, I mean."

I was idly watching my stepfather. The sun was beating down on us kind of hard, and it was difficult to think about anything except how much I wished I were at the beach.

"I don't know," I said. I could understand Shannon's pain, of course. She had a crush on a guy. All she wanted to know was whether or not she was wasting her time.

As the sister of the object of her affections, however, all I could think was . . . *ew*. Also, that David is *way* too young to have a girlfriend.

"One of the members of the historical society—don't think I don't see you there, Bob," Andy went on laughingly, "even ventured that this belt buckle might have belonged to someone in the Diego clan, a very old, very respected family that settled in this area nearly two hundred years ago."

Respected, my butt. The Diegos—or at least, the ghosts of the two members of the family I had had the misfortune to meet—had all been thieves and murderers.

"I believe that for that reason and not just because of its intricate beauty," Andy continued, "this piece is going to be highly sought after by collectors someday . . . and, who knows, maybe even today!"

"David doesn't really talk about girls at home all that much," I said to Shannon. "At least, not to me."

"Oh." Shannon looked dejected. "But do you think . . . well, do you think if Dave *did* like a girl, it'd be, you know, someone like me?"

"Let's start the bidding for this fine piece of authentic period jewelry at a hundred dollars," Andy said. "A hundred dollars. Okay, we have a hundred. How about a hundred and twenty-five? Does anybody bid a hundred and twenty-five?"

I thought about what Shannon had asked me. *David, a girlfriend?* The youngest of my stepbrothers, I could no more picture David with a girlfriend than I could picture him behind the wheel of a car or even playing soccer. He just isn't that kind of guy.

"Three fifty," I heard Andy say. "Do I hear three fifty?"

But I supposed that one day David *would* drive a car. I

mean, *I* could drive now, and there'd been a time when my whole family had despaired of *that* ever happening. It made sense that someday David would be sixteen and do all the same things that his older brothers Jake and Brad and I were doing. . . . You know, drive. Take trig. Make out with members of the opposite sex.

"My goodness, Bob," Andy said into the microphone. "You weren't kidding when you mentioned how important you thought this piece was going to be to our auction today, were you? I have seven hundred dollars. Does anyone— Okay, seven fifty. Do I hear eight?"

"Sure," I said to Shannon. "I mean, why *wouldn't* David like you? I mean, if he liked anyone better than anybody else. Which I'm not saying he does. That I know of."

"Really?" Shannon looked worried. "Because Dave's really smart. And I think he'd probably only like smart girls. But I'm not doing all that well in math."

"I'm sure David wouldn't care about something like that," I said even though I wasn't sure of it at all. "So long as, you know, you're a nice person, and all."

"Really?" Shannon flushed prettily. "Do you really think so?"

My God, what had I said?

Fortunately at that moment, Andy brought his auctioneer's hammer down hard, and distracted Shannon by shouting, "Sold for eleven hundred dollars!"

"Wow," Shannon said. "That's a lot of money."

She wasn't the only one in shock. There was an astonished hum through the crowd. Eleven hundred dollars was the most any item on the block had brought in so far. I craned my neck to see what kind of fool had that much money to burn on a piece of junk, and was a little startled to see that Andy was still holding up the belt buckle Jake had found in the attic . . .

. . . and that Paul Slater, of all people, was striding up through the crowd to claim it.

I watched as Paul, looking pleased, shook Andy's hand, took the belt buckle, then whipped out his checkbook. *What a loser*, I thought. I mean, I had known Paul was a weirdo for a long time. But to throw away his hard-earned money—well, not so hard-earned, actually, because I was pretty sure he was paying for the belt buckle with funds stolen from the Gutierrezes—on a piece of junk like that. . . . Well, that was just insane.

It didn't make any sense. Why would Paul Slater spend 1,100 bucks on a banged-up old belt buckle . . . even if it *had* been polished and its linage could be traced back to its original owner, someone in the Diego clan?

And then, as if someone had brought Andy's auctioneer's hammer down on my head, finally banging some sense into me, it all became clear.

And I began to feel as if I might throw up all those baked goods we'd secretly been scarfing down behind Sister Ernestine's back. I guess it must have shown on my face, since Shannon suddenly sucked in her breath and went, "Are you all right?"

"Bad lemon bar," I said. "I'll be right back." I got up and hurried away from the bake sale table, around the back of the rows of folding chairs, and then up the aisle, toward the dais where Paul was standing, collecting his bounty.

But before I could get anywhere close to him, someone grabbed me by the arm.

My heart was beating so fast on account of the whole Paul-trying-to-keep-my-boyfriend-from-dying thing, that I almost jumped a mile in the air, I was so startled.

But it turned out it was only my mother.

"Susie, honey," she said, smiling beatifically up at Andy, behind his podium. "Isn't this fun? Isn't Andy doing great?"

"Uh," I said, "yeah, Mom."

"He's a real natural, isn't he?" She's so in love with this guy. It's totally gross. In, like, a nice way, I guess. But still gross.

"Yeah," I said. "Look, I have to—"

But I shouldn't have worried. Because Paul found me.

"Suze," he said, coming down the steps from the dais. I was too late. The transaction had been completed. In his hand was the belt buckle. "Fancy meeting you here."

"I need to talk to you," I said more intensely than I'd meant to, because both my mother and Sister Ernestine, who was standing nearby with Paul's check still hot in her hands, turned to look at me.

"Susie, honey," my mom said. "You all right?"

"I'm fine," I said quickly. Could they tell? Could they tell my heart was hammering a mile a minute and that my mouth was as dry as sand? "I just need to talk to Paul really fast."

"And who is minding the bake sale table?" Sister Ernestine wanted to know.

"Shannon's got it under control," I said, reaching out and taking Paul's arm. He was watching us—my mom, Sister Ernestine, and me—with a slightly sardonic smile, as if everything we were saying was amusing him very much.

"Well, don't leave her alone too long," Sister Ernestine said severely. I could tell that wasn't what she'd wanted to say, but just as far as she was willing to go in front of my mom.

"I won't, Sister," I said.

And then I dragged Paul away from the dais and folding chairs, and over behind one of the display tables holding the rest of the stuff that was to be auctioned.

"What do you think you're doing?" I hissed at him the moment we were out of earshot.

"Well, hey, Suze," he said, looking as if he were still finding plenty about the situation to amuse him. "Nice to see you, too."

"Don't give me that," I said. It was kind of hard to talk with my mouth feeling so dry and all, but I wasn't about to give up. "What did you buy that belt buckle for?"

"This?" Paul opened his fist and I saw silver flash in the bright sun for a second before his fingers closed over it again. "Oh, I don't know. I just thought it was pretty."

"Eleven hundred dollars' worth of pretty?" I glared at him, hoping he couldn't see how badly I was shaking. "Come on, Paul, I'm not stupid. I know why you bought that thing."

"Really?" Paul's grin was more infuriating than ever. "Enlighten me."

"Only it's not going to work." My heart was slamming into my ribs now, but I knew there was no going back. "Jesse's last name is de Silva. That's an *S*, not a *D*. That isn't his buckle."

I'd expected this news to wipe the insufferable smile right off Paul's face.

Only it didn't. The corners of his mouth didn't even waver.

"I know it isn't Jesse's buckle," he said evenly. "Anything else, Suze? Or can I go now?"

I stared at him. I could feel my pulse slowing down, and the roaring sound that had filled my ears since I'd realized he was the buckle's new owner suddenly disappeared. For the first time in several minutes, I was able to take a deep breath. Before, I'd only been able to manage shallow ones.

"Then . . . then you know," I said, feeling ridiculously relieved, "you know you won't be able to use that to go . . . to go back through time to save Jesse."

"Of course," Paul said, his smile growing broader than ever. "Because I'm going to use it to go back through time to stop Jesse's murderer. See you, Suze."

chapter *ten*

Diego. Felix Diego, the man who'd killed Jesse, because Jesse's fiancée, the heinous Maria, asked him to. She had wanted to marry Diego, a slave-runner and mercenary, rather than the man her father had picked out for her to marry, her cousin (*ew*) Jesse.

But Jesse never made it to the wedding. That's because he was killed on his way there. Killed by Felix Diego, though no one at the time knew that. His body was never found. People—Jesse's own family, even—assumed that he'd chosen to run away rather than marry a girl he didn't love and who didn't love him. Maria had gone on to marry Felix, and they'd produced a whole bunch of kids who later grew up to be murderers and thieves themselves.

And, not too long ago, the pair of them had paid a little visit to me, at Paul's behest. He'd met Diego's ghost. In fact, Paul was the one who'd summoned him.

Now Paul was going to stop Diego from killing Jesse . . .

probably by killing Diego himself. It's easy for shifters to kill people. All we have to do is remove their souls from their bodies, escort them to that spiritual way station where their fate—whatever it was, heaven, hell, next life—was decided, and boom: back on earth, another unexplained death, another body in the morgue.

Or, in Diego's case, the icehouse, because they didn't have morgues in California circa 1850.

Except that it wasn't going to happen like that. I wasn't going to let Paul do it. Oh sure, Diego deserved to die. He was the scum of the earth. He'd killed my boyfriend, after all.

But if Diego died, that meant Jesse wouldn't.

And then I'd never meet him.

I knew, of course, that I couldn't stop Paul on my own—short of killing him myself. I needed backup.

Fortunately, I knew just where to find it. As soon as the auction was over, and Sister Ernestine dismissed Shannon and me with a curt, "You may go now," I booked for my mom's car, which she'd graciously allowed me to borrow for the day, in light of my "volunteering" to help out at the Mission. Paul had left the second after he'd dropped his little bomb about stopping Felix Diego. I had no way of knowing, really, where he'd disappeared to.

But I had a pretty good idea who might know.

The sun was just starting to set as I pulled out onto Scenic Drive, painting the western sky a deep burnt orange, and turning the sea the color of flames. The windows in the expensive seaside homes I passed reflected the light from the setting sun, so you couldn't see inside them.

But I knew that behind the glowing glass, families were just sitting down to dinner . . . families like my own. I was going to be in big trouble for what I was doing . . . not for trying to keep Paul from saving my boyfriend's life, but for missing dinner. Andy's a real stickler about family meal-times.

But what choice did I have? There was a life at stake here. And okay, so the life belonged to a heinous killer who deserved to die. That was beside the point. Paul had to be stopped.

And I knew of only one person he might possibly listen to.

But when I pulled into the Slaters' driveway, I saw that my panic had been for nothing. Not only was Paul's silver BMW convertible there, but it had been joined by a red Porsche Boxster that I recognized only too well.

Paul wouldn't, I knew, be hurtling through alternative dimensions any time soon.

I parked behind the Boxster, then hurried up the long flight of stone steps to the modern house's front door, where I leaned on the bell. A cool, crisp breeze was blowing in from the sea. Inhaling it, you almost felt like all was right with the world . . . anything that could smell that clean and fresh had to be good, right?

Wrong. So wrong. The water in Carmel Bay can be treach-erous, with dangerous riptides that had swept hundreds of hapless vacationers to their deaths. It was fitting that Paul would live just yards away from something so deadly.

Paul answered the door himself. You could tell he was expecting some kind of food delivery, and not me, because he had his wallet out.

To his credit, when he saw it was me, and not, say, my stepbrother Jake delivering a pie from Peninsula Pizza, Paul didn't skip a beat. He slipped his wallet back into the pocket of his perfectly pressed chinos and said with a slow smile, "Suze. To what do I owe the pleasure?"

"Don't get your hopes up," I said. With luck he'd mistake my sudden hoarseness for gruff disconcern, and not what it actually was, which was fear. "I'm not here to see you."

"Paul?" A familiar voice tinkled like wind chimes from somewhere deep in the house. "Make sure he gives you extra of those, you know. Whaddyacallems. Hot sprinkles."

Paul looked over his shoulder, and I saw Kelly Prescott—barefoot, with the straps of her extremely skimpy Betsey Johnson dress slipping off her shoulders—coming down the stairs.

"Oh," she said when she saw it was me at the door and not a pizza. "Suze. What are *you* doing here?"

"Sorry to interrupt," I said, hoping they couldn't see how fast my heart was racing beneath the conservative white blouse I'd worn to appease Sister Ernestine. "But I really need to have a word with Paul's grandfather."

"Grandpa Gork?" Kelly looked up at Paul inquisitively. "You told me he couldn't talk!"

"Apparently," Paul said, the amused smile never leaving his face, "he does. But only to Suze."

Kelly flicked a scathing glance at me. "Geez, Suze," she said. "I didn't know you were so into old people."

"That's me," I said with a laugh I hoped didn't sound as nervous to their ears as it did to my own. "Friend to the old people. So . . . can I come in?"

I half expected Paul to say no. I mean, he had to have known why I was there. He had to have known I only wanted to talk to Dr. Slaski so I could see if he knew of some way I could stop his grandson from playing with the past . . . and messing up my present.

But instead of looking angry about it or even mildly annoyed, Paul opened the door wider and said, "Be my guest."

I stepped inside and managed a smile at Kelly as I went by her and up the stairs to the main floor. Kelly didn't return the smile. I could see why when I stepped into the living room. There was a fire going in the fireplace and, from the placement of the brandy snifters on the chrome-and-glass coffee table in front of the long low couch, it appeared that I'd interrupted a "moment" between her and Paul.

I tried not to take it personally that Paul had never broken out the brandy or firewood during the many times I'd been over. I am, after all, taken. Still, the whole thing smacked of overkill. Kelly had been warm for Paul's form for so long, she'd have been happy with beef jerky and a Slurpee, let alone a fire and Courvoisier.

I hurried past the living room and down the long hallway that led to Dr. Slaski's room. I could hear the Game

Show Network blaring away. That must have been a nice accompaniment to Kelly and Paul's make-out session. The dulcet tones of Bob Barker. *Smack, smack.*

When I got to Dr. Slaski's room, I stopped and knocked, just to make sure I wasn't interrupting a sponge bath or anything. When no one called for me to come in, I went ahead and pushed the partly open door. Dr. Slaski's attendant was sprawled in a chair in one corner, taking what was probably a well-earned nap. Dr. Slaski himself, propped up in his hospital bed, appeared to be dozing as well.

I hated to wake him, of course, but what choice did I have? Was I wrong in thinking that he might want to know that his own grandson was thinking of tampering with the course of history, something he himself had warned me was perilous in the extreme?

"Dr. Slaski?" I whispered, since I didn't want to wake the attendant, as well. "Dr. Slaski? Are you awake? It's me, Suze. Suze Simon. I have something really important I need to ask you."

Dr. Slaski opened one eye and looked at me. "This," he wheezed—his breathing didn't sound right— "had better be good."

"It's not," I assured him. "I mean, it's not good news, anyway. It's about Paul."

Dr. Slaski looked toward the ceiling. "Why am I not surprised?"

"It's just," I said, slipping onto the chair beside his bed, "that I found out why Paul wants to go back through time."

Dr. Slaski's eyelids opened a little wider. "To save

mankind from the atrocities of Stalin?" he rasped.

"Um," I said. "No. To keep my boyfriend from dying."

Paul's grandfather blinked his rheumy eyes at me. "And this is a bad thing because . . . ?"

"Because if Paul goes back through time and saves Jesse," I whispered, to keep the attendant from overhearing, "I'll never meet him!"

"Paul?"

"No." I couldn't believe this. "*Jesse!*"

Dr. Slaski licked his cracked lips. "Because," he wheezed, "Jesse is . . ."

"Dead, all right?" I shot the still-dozing attendant a careful look. "Jesse is dead. My boyfriend is a ghost."

Slowly, Dr. Slaski closed his eyes. "I don't," he sighed, "have the patience for this. I'm not feeling very well today."

"Dr. Slaski!" I leaned forward and prodded his arm. "Please, you have to help me. Tell Paul he can't do this. Tell him he can't play around with time travel, the way you told me. Tell him it's dangerous, that he'll end up like you. Tell him something, *anything*. But you've got to get him to stop before he ruins my life!"

Dr. Slaski, his eyes still closed, shook his head slowly from side to side. "You've come to the wrong person," he said. "I can't control that boy. Never could. Never will."

"But you can still *try*, Dr. Slaski," I cried. "Please, you've *got* to! If he saves Jesse . . . if he succeeds . . ."

"Your heart will break." Dr. Slaski had opened his eyes and was gazing at me. "Your life will be over."

"Yes!"

"How old are you?" Dr. Slaski wanted to know. "Fifteen? Sixteen? You really think your life will be over if a boy you have a crush on—not even a boy, a *ghost*!—happens to disappear? Next year, you wouldn't remember him, anyway."

"That isn't true," I hissed at him through gritted teeth. "What Jesse and I have . . . it's something special. Paul knows that. That's why he's trying to ruin it."

Dr. Slaski looked interested in that.

"Is he?" he said with a little more animation. "And why would he want to do that, do you think?"

"Because . . ." I was embarrassed to admit it, but what choice did I have, really? I took a deep breath. "Because he thinks we should be together. Him and me. Because we're mediators."

A slow smile broke out across Dr. Slaski's dry, liver-spotted lips.

"Shifters," he corrected me.

"Shifters," I said. "Whatever. Dr. Slaski, it's not right, and you know it."

"On the contrary," Dr. Slaski said with a phlegmy cough. "It's probably the smartest thing that boy's ever done. Romantic, too. Almost gives me faith in him."

"Dr. Slaski!"

"What's so wrong with it, anyway?" Dr. Slaski glared at me. "Sounds to me like he's doing you a favor. Or the boyfriend, anyway. You think this Jessup—"

"Jesse."

"You think this Jesse likes being a ghost? Hanging around for all eternity, watching you live your life, while he hovers in the background, never aging, never feeling an ocean breeze on his face, never again tasting blueberry pie. Is that the kind of life you wish for him? You must love him a lot, if that's true."

I felt heat rising in my cheeks at his tone.

"Of course that's not what I want for him," I said fiercely. "But if the alternative is never having known him at all—well, I don't want that, either. And neither would he!"

"But you haven't asked him, have you?"

"Well, I—"

"Have you?"

"Well." I looked down, unable to meet his gaze. "No. No, I haven't."

"I didn't think so," Dr. Slaski said. "And I know why, too. You're afraid of what he'll say. You're afraid he'll say he'd rather live."

I looked up sharply. "That isn't true!"

"It is and you know it. You're afraid he'd say he'd rather live out the rest of his life, the way he was supposed to, never having known you—"

"There has to be another way!" I cried. "It can't just be one thing or the other. Paul said something about soul transference—"

"Ah," Dr. Slaski said. "But for that, you need to have a body available to take the soul you want to transfer into it."

I thought darkly of Paul. "I think I know of one," I said.

As if he'd read my thoughts, Dr. Slaski said, "But you won't do that."

I raised my eyebrows. "Won't I?"

"No," he said. His voice was beginning to sound fainter and fainter. "No, you won't. *He* would. If he thought it'd get him what he wanted. But not you. You don't have it in you."

"I *do*," I said as fiercely as I was able.

But Dr. Slaski only shook his head again. "You're not like him," he said. "Or me. No need to get huffy about it. It's a good thing. You'll live longer."

"Maybe," I said, tears filling my eyes as I looked down at my hands. "But what's the point, if I'm not happy?"

Dr. Slaski didn't say anything for a while. His breathing had grown so raspy, that after a minute or so, I began to think he was snoring, and looked up, fearing he'd fallen asleep.

But he hadn't. His gaze on me was steady.

"You love this boy?" Dr. Slaski asked finally.

"Jesse?" I nodded, unable to say more.

"There is *one* thing you could do," he wheezed. "Never tried it myself, but I heard it could be done. Wouldn't recommend it, of course. Probably put you into an early grave, like I'll be, soon enough."

I leaned forward in my chair.

"What is it?" I cried. "Tell me, please. I'll do anything . . . anything!"

"Anything that doesn't involve killing someone, you mean," Dr. Slaski said and broke down into a coughing fit from which it seemed to take him ages to recover. Finally, lying back on his hospital bed, the horrible, body-wracking spasms finished, he wheezed, "When you go back . . ."

"Back? Through time, you mean?"

He didn't respond. He just looked up at the ceiling.

"Dr. Slaski? Go back through time? Is that what you meant?"

But Dr. Slaski never finished that sentence. Because midway through it, his jaw went slack, his eyes closed, and he fell sound asleep.

Or at least that's what I assumed.

I couldn't believe it. He's about to give me some really valuable tip on how I might be able to save Jesse, and suddenly his Excedrin PM kicks in? What's the deal with *that*?

I reached out to touch his hand, hoping that might wake him. "Dr. Slaski?" I called a little more loudly. When he still didn't respond, panic set in.

"Dr. Slaski?" I cried. "Dr. Slaski, wake up!"

My scream brought the attendant snorting back into consciousness. He was up and out of his chair at once, crying, "What? What is it?"

"I don't know," I stammered. "He—he won't wake up."

The attendant's fingers flew over Paul's grandfather's body, feeling for a pulse, adjusting IVs . . .

Next thing I knew, he'd straddled the old man and was pounding on his chest.

"Call nine-one-one," he yelled at me.

I just stood there, not understanding. "He was just talking to me," I said. "We were having a totally normal conversation. I mean, he was coughing a lot, but . . . but he was fine. And then all of a sudden—"

The attendant had to say it twice.

"Call 911! Get an ambulance!"

That's when I noticed that there was a phone right there in the room. I picked it up and dialed. When the operator came on, I told her that we needed an ambulance and gave her the address. Meanwhile, behind me, the attendant had placed an oxygen mask over Dr. Slaski's face, and was filling a syringe with something.

"I don't understand this," he kept saying. "He was fine an hour ago. Just fine!"

I didn't understand it, either. Unless Dr. Slaski was much more ill than he'd ever let on.

There didn't seem to be much else I could do to help, so I figured I'd better go and tell Paul his grandfather had had some sort of attack. I got back to the living room just in time to see Kelly, seated beside Paul on the couch, her legs draped over his like a throw, stick her tongue in his mouth. . . . A sight I actually would have paid money to have been spared.

"Ahem," I said, from the hallway.

Kelly pulled her face off Paul's and looked at me sourly.

"What do *you* want?" she demanded. Given her animosity toward me, you'd hardly have guessed that we were currently president and vice president of the junior class, and had to work daily (well, weekly) together in order to decide such important issues as where to go for a class trip and what kind of flowers to order for the spring formal.

Ignoring Kelly, I said, "Paul, your grandfather appears to be having a heart attack or something."

Paul looked at me through eyes that were half lidded. That Kelly sure has some sucking power.

"What?" he said stupidly.

"Your grandfather." I lifted a hand to push some hair from my eyes. I hoped he didn't notice how much my fingers were shaking. "An ambulance is on the way. He's had like a stroke or something."

Paul didn't look surprised. He said, "Oh," in kind of a disappointed voice . . . but more like he was bummed that his make-out session with Kelly had been interrupted than that his grandfather was, for all we knew, dying.

"Be right there," Paul said and started to disentangle himself from Kelly's legs.

"Paul," Kelly cried. She managed to give his name two syllables, so it came out sounding like *Paw-wol*.

"Sorry, Kel," Paul said, giving one of her calves a good-natured pat. "Grandpa Gork's OD'd on his meds again. Gotta go take care of business."

Kelly pouted prettily. "But the pizza's not even here yet!"

"We'll have to take a rain check, babe," he said.

Babe. I shuddered.

Then realized what he'd said. As he moved past me to get to his grandfather's room, I reached out and seized his arm. "What do you mean, he's OD'd on his meds?" I hissed.

"Uh," Paul said, looking down at me with a half smile. "Because that's what happened?"

"How do you know? You haven't even seen him yet!"

"Uh," he said, the smile growing broader. "Because maybe I helped make it happen."

I dropped my hand as if his skin had suddenly burst into flames. "*You* did this?" I couldn't believe what I was hearing.

Except that I should have. I really should have. Because it was Paul.

"For God's sake, Paul, *why?*"

"I knew you'd be coming over to see him after what happened today at the auction," he said with a shrug. "And frankly, I didn't need the hassle from the old man. Now if you'll excuse me . . ."

He went sauntering down the hall in the direction of his grandfather's room. I stared after him, not quite believing what I'd just heard.

And yet . . .

And yet it made sense. It was Paul, after all. Paul, a guy whose morals were more than a little askew.

Feeling numb, I wandered back out into the living room, where Kelly was pulling on her shoes and squawking into her cell phone. "No, I'm telling you, she came busting in here, demanding to know what I was doing with *her* boyfriend. Well, okay, she didn't say it *quite* like that. She made up some story about wanting to talk to Paul's grandfather. Yeah, I know, the one who can't talk. I know, have you ever heard a lamer excuse? Then she—" Looking up, Kelly saw me. "Oh, sorry, Deb, gotta go, call you later." She hung up and just stood there, glaring at me. "Thanks," she said finally, "for spoiling what otherwise might have been a really nice evening."

I was tempted to tell her the truth—that I hadn't spoiled anything. Paul was the one who'd apparently overmedicated his grandfather. At least, that seemed to be what he wanted me to believe.

But what would have been the point? She wouldn't have believed me, anyway.

"Sorry," was all I said, and started for the door.

When I opened it, however, I saw my stepbrother Jake standing there, a pizza box in his hand.

"Peninsula Pizza, that'll be twenty-seven ninety . . ." His voice trailed off as he recognized me. "Suze? What are *you* doing here?"

"Just leaving," I said.

"Yeah, well, you'd better." Jake glanced at his watch. "You're gonna be late for dinner. Dad'll kill you."

Yet another thing to look forward to.

"Kelly," I called up the stairs. "Your pizza's here!" To Jake I said, "Hope you remembered the hot pepper flakes."

Then I left.

chapter *eleven*

Because of the auction, Andy was late putting dinner on the table, so I ended up getting home just in time. My mom couldn't understand why I was so quiet during the meal, though. She thought maybe I'd gotten too much sun sitting out at the bake sale table.

"Sister Ernestine should at least have given you an umbrella," she said as she dug into the pork tenderloin Andy had prepared. "That little girl you were sitting with . . . what was her name again?"

"Shannon."

Only it wasn't me who said it. It was David.

"Yes, Shannon," my mother said. "She's a redhead, like David. That much sun can be very damaging to redheads. I hope she was wearing sunscreen."

I half expected David to come up with one of his usual comments—you know, the exact statistical incidents of skin cancer occurring in eighth graders in northern

California, or something. His head was filled with all sorts of useless information like that. Instead, he just flicked his mashed potatoes around his plate, until Brad, who'd finished all of his own mashed potatoes, as well as what was left in the bowl, went, "Man, are you going to eat that or play with it? Because if you don't want it, give it to me."

"David," Andy said. "Finish what's on your plate."

David picked up a spoonful of mashed potatoes and ate it.

Brad's gaze immediately flickered over to my plate. But the hopeful look in his eye faded when he saw how clean it was. Not, of course, that I'd felt like eating. At all.

But I had Max, the family dog-slash-garbage disposal, by my side, and I'd grown expert at slipping him what I couldn't choke down myself.

"May I be excused?" I asked. "I think maybe I did get a little too much sun—"

"It's Suze's turn to put the plates in the dishwasher," Brad declared.

"No, it isn't." I couldn't believe this. Didn't these people realize I had *way* more important things to do than worry about household chores? I had to make sure my boyfriend died, like he was supposed to. "I did it last week."

"Nuh-uh," Brad said. "You and Jake traded weeks, remember? Because he had to work the dinner shift this week."

Since this was indisputably true—I'd seen the evidence myself over at Paul's—I couldn't argue anymore.

"Fine," I said, scooting my chair back, nearly running

over Max in the process, and standing up. "I'll do it."

"Thank you, Susie," my mom said with a smile as I took her plate.

My reply wasn't exactly gracious. I muttered, "Whatever," and went into the kitchen with everybody's plates, Max following closely at my heels. Max loves it when I have plate-clearing duty, because I just scrape everything into his bowl, rather than into the trash compactor.

But on that night, Max and I weren't alone in the kitchen.

Even though I didn't notice anyone else in there right away, I knew something was up when Max suddenly lifted his head from his bowl and fled, his food only half finished, and his tail between his legs. Only one thing had the power to make Max leave pork uneaten, and that was a visitor from beyond.

He materialized a second later.

"Hey, kiddo," he said. "How's it going?"

I didn't scream or anything. I just poured Lemon Joy into the pot Andy had used to cook the potatoes, then filled it with hot water.

"Nice timing, Dad," I said. "You just stop by to say hi, or did someone on the ghost grapevine alert you to my extreme mental anguish?"

He smiled. He looked no different than he had the day he died. . . . No different from the dozens of times he'd visited me since then. He was still wearing the shirt he'd died in—the shirt I'd slept with for so many years.

"I heard you were having some . . . issues," my dad said.

That's the problem with ghosts. When they aren't haunting people, they sit around in the spectral plane, gossiping. Dad had even met Jesse. . . . A prospect I found too horrifying to even contemplate sometimes.

And of course, when you're dead . . . well . . . there isn't a whole lot to do. I knew my dad spent a goodly portion of his free time basically spying on me.

"Been a while since we had a chat," Dad went on, looking around the kitchen appreciatively. His gaze fell on the sliding glass doors and he noticed the hot tub. He whistled appreciatively. "That's new."

"Andy built it," I said. I started in on the glass dish Andy had roasted the pork in.

"Is there anything that guy can't do?" my dad wanted to know. But he was, I knew, being sarcastic. My dad doesn't like Andy. At least, not that much.

"No," I said. "Andy is a man of many talents. And I don't know what you've seen—or heard—but I'm fine, Dad. Really."

"Wouldn't expect you to be anything else." My dad looked more closely at the kitchen counters. "Is that real granite? Or imitation?"

"Dad." I nearly threw the dish towel at him. "Quit stalling and say what you came to say. Because if it's what I think you're here to say, no deal."

"And what do you think that is?" Dad wanted to know, folding his arms and leaning back against the kitchen counter.

"I'm not going to let him do it, Dad," I said. "I'm not."

My dad sighed. Not because he was sad. He sighed with happiness. In life, Dad had been a lawyer. In death, he still relished a good argument.

"Jesse deserves another chance," he said. "I know it. You know it."

"If he doesn't die," I said, attacking the potato pot with perhaps more energy than was strictly necessary, "I'll never meet him. Same with you."

Dad raised his eyebrows. "Same with . . . oh, you mean you thought about saving me?" He looked pleased. "Suze, that's the sweetest thing you've ever said to me."

That did it. Just those ten little words. Suddenly, something inside of me seemed to break, and a second later, I was sobbing in his arms . . . only silently, so no one else in the house could hear.

"Oh, Dad," I wept into his shirtfront. "I don't know what to do. I want to bring you back. I do, I really do."

Dad stroked my hair and said in the kindest voice imaginable, "I know. I know you do, kiddo."

That just made me cry harder. "But if I save you," I choked, "I'll never meet *him*."

"I know," my dad said again. "Susie, I know."

"What should I do, Dad?" I asked, lifting my head from his chest and attempting to control myself—his shirt was practically soaked already. "I'm so confused. Help me. Please."

"Susie." Dad grinned down at me, still tenderly brushing back my hair with his hands. "I never thought I'd see the day when you, of all people, would actually admit you need help. Especially from me."

I used a fist to swipe at the tears that were still rolling down my face. "Of course I need you, Dad," I whispered. "I've always needed you. I always will."

"I don't know about that." My dad, instead of stroking my hair, rumpled it now. "But I do know one thing. This time-shifting thing. It's dangerous?"

I sniffled. "Well," I said. "Yeah."

"And do you really think," Dad went on, the skin around his eyes crinkling, "that I'd let my little girl risk her life to save mine?"

"But, Dad—"

"No, Suze." The crinkles deepened and I could tell he was more serious than he'd been in a long time. "Not for me. I'd give anything to live again"—and now I saw that, along with the crinkles, there was moisture there, as well— "but not if it means anything bad might happen to you."

I gazed up at him, my eyes as bright with tears as his own. "Oh, Dad," I said, unable to keep the throb from my throat.

He reached up to lay a hand on either side of my wet face. "And I wouldn't presume to speak for Jesse," he said, tilting my head so that we were looking straight into each other's eyes. "But I think I can safely say that he's not going to like the idea of you risking your life to save his any more than I do. Knowing him, in fact, he'll probably like it even less."

I reached up and placed my hands over his own. Then I said, "I get it, Dad. Really, I do. And I won't go back for you if you really don't want me to. But . . . I still can't let him do it, Dad. Paul, I mean."

"Can't let him save the life of the guy you supposedly love," Dad said, not looking too happy to hear it. "Something's very wrong with that picture, Suze."

"I know, Dad," I said, "but I love him. You know it. You can't ask me to just sit back and let Paul do this. If he succeeds I won't even remember having *met* Jesse."

"Right," my dad said reasonably. "So it won't hurt."

"It *will*," I insisted, "It *will* hurt, Dad. Because deep down, I'll know. I'll know there was someone . . . someone I was supposed to have met. Only I'll never meet him. I'll go through my whole life waiting for him to come along, only he never will. What kind of life is that, Dad, huh? What kind of life is *that*?"

"And what kind of life," my dad asked gently, "is it for Jesse to spend all of eternity as a ghost—especially if something goes wrong and you end up dead right along with him?"

"Then," I said with a feeble attempt at humor, "at least we'll be able to haunt people together for the rest of eternity."

"With Jesse having to live forever with the guilt of knowing he's the reason you died in the first place? I don't think so, Suze."

He had me there. I stared up at him, unable to think of a single thing to say in reply.

"Suze, your whole life," my dad went on, not without sympathy, "you've always made the right decisions. Not necessarily the easiest ones. The right ones. Don't mess that up now, when you're facing what's probably the most important decision you'll ever have to make."

I opened my mouth to tell him he was wrong . . . that I was making the right decision . . . that I was doing what I knew Jesse would want . . .

Only I knew there was no point.

So instead I said, "All right, Dad. But there's just one thing I don't understand."

He nodded. "Why Maroon 5 is so popular?"

"Um," I said, grinning in spite of myself. "No. I don't understand why, if you feel that way . . . that you had a good life and that you've learned so much since you died . . . If you really feel that way, then why are you still here?"

"You should know," he said.

I blinked at him. "I should? How?"

"Because you said it yourself."

"When did I—"

"Um . . . Suze?"

I whirled around and found myself looking not into my dad's gentle brown eyes but David's anxious blue ones.

"Are you okay?" David's pale face was pinched with concern. "Were you . . . were you just crying?"

"Of course not," I said, hastily snatching up a dish towel—seeing, as I did so, that my dad had vanished—and scrubbing my cheeks with it. "I'm fine. What's up?"

"Um . . . " David looked around the kitchen, his eyes wide. "Are you . . . are you not alone?"

Outside of my dad, David is the only one in my family who knows the truth about me . . . or at least, most of the truth. If I had told him all of it . . . well, he'd probably be able to handle it, with his scientific, orderly mind.

But I don't think he'd have liked it.

"I am now," I said, knowing what he meant.

"I just came in for dessert," David said. "Dad said . . . Dad said he made a fruit tart."

"Right," I said. "Well. I'm through here. I'll just be going upstairs."

I turned to go, but David's voice—it had changed lately, gone from squeaky to deep in the course of a few months— stopped me by the door. "Suze. Are you sure you're all right? You seem . . . sad."

"Sad?" I looked back at him over my shoulder. "I'm not sad. Well, not that sad. Just . . . there's just something I have to do." Because I had already decided that, despite my dad's concerns, I wasn't giving Jesse up just yet. Not without a fight. "Something I'm not exactly looking forward to."

"Oh," David said. Then his face brightened. "Then just do it quick. You know, like pulling off a Band-Aid."

Do it quick. I'd have loved to. But I had no way of knowing when Paul was going to make his trip back through time. For all I knew, I could wake up tomorrow with no memory of Jesse whatsoever.

"Thanks," I said to David, managing a semblance of a smile. "I'll keep that in mind."

But I wasn't smiling a half hour later, when I finally managed to get Father Dominic—my last hope—on the phone.

Father Dom wasn't exactly as sympathetic to my plight as I'd hoped he be. I'd thought the information I had to impart—about Paul buying Felix Diego's belt buckle, and then possibly drugging his own grandfather—would spark a little righteous indignation in the old guy.

But Father Dominic's sentiments seemed right in line with my dad's. Jesse had died too young, too violently. He had a right to a second chance at life. It was morally reprehensible of me to stand in the way of that.

Maybe Father D. had other reasons to be feeling upbeat. The monsignor had come out of his coma and seemed to be recuperating nicely.

"Huh," I said as Father D. imparted this supposedly joyous news. "That's great, Father D. Now, about Paul—"

"I wouldn't worry too much about it, Susannah," he said. "I'll admit it was wrong, what he did to his grandfather—if, indeed, he really did—"

"He said he did, Father D.," I interrupted. "Well, almost."

"Yes," Father Dominic said. "Well, the two of you do have a tendency to, er, exaggerate the truth somewhat—"

"Father Dom," I said, my fingers tightening on the receiver. "I called the ambulance myself."

"So you said. Still, Susannah, for Paul to do this thing—this time-travel thing you spoke of—I understand he'd have to put himself in the exact spot where the person he wishes to see was once standing during the exact time he wishes to travel back to."

"Yeah," I said. "So?" I wasn't usually so rude to Father

Dom, but this was, you have to admit, an extenuating circumstance.

"So wouldn't that mean Paul would have to travel from your bedroom?" Father Dominic sounded a bit distracted. That's because he was. He was packing to come back home. He was planning on driving back to Carmel that very night. "Isn't that where Diego killed Jesse? Your room? It's rather unlikely Paul is going to be able to get into your bedroom, Susannah," he went on. "Not without your permission."

I nearly dropped the phone. I couldn't believe it. I couldn't believe this hadn't occurred to me before.

Because Father Dominic was right. There was no way Paul was traveling back to the night Jesse died . . . not unless he did a little breaking and entering. Because that was the only way he was getting into my room. The *only* way.

"I hadn't thought of that," I said with a growing feeling of relief. "But you're right. Oh my God, you're totally right. Father Dominic, you're a genius!"

"Er," Father Dominic said. "Thank you, Susannah. I suppose. Although if you were to do the right thing, you'd allow Paul in and let Jesse live out his life naturally, as he was meant to—"

"Um," I said. I'd heard this tune before, one too many times. Fortunately, the call-waiting went off at that very moment. Perfect timing.

"Oops, that's my other line, Father D.," I said. "Gotta go. See you when you get back."

I hung up the phone, feeling better than I had since . . .

well, since the auction that afternoon. Jesse was safe. Paul couldn't make him disappear, because to do so, he'd have to have access to my bedroom. How else was he going to find his way back to 1850?

He needed to have a place to stand, somewhere that existed in both 1850 and the present. Somewhere Felix Diego had once stood. Where was he going to go? The mall?

"Hello?" I said, clicking over to the other call.

"Suze?" It was CeeCee, sounding breathless with excitement. "Oh my God, you'll never believe what just happened."

"What?" I asked, not actually paying attention. Because, really, where else could Paul go, if not my bedroom?

"He asked me." CeeCee's voice was actually trembling. "Adam. Adam asked me to the Winter Formal. We're just at the Coffee Clutch, you know, having cappuccinos—we'd have asked you, only I know you were at the auction all day—"

"Uh-huh," I said.

"—and he just asked me. Out of the blue. I had to run outside and call you. He's still inside. I just . . . Oh, my God. I had to tell someone. He asked me."

Besides, it isn't like Paul is going to be able to do it anytime soon, anyway. Go back through time, I mean. Not with his grandfather in the hospital.

"That is so great, CeeCee," I said into the phone.

"I guess I should go back in and say yes," CeeCee said. "I should say yes, right? Or should I play hard to get? I don't want him to think I'm too eager. And it *is* next weekend.

Technically, he should have asked me a long time ago—"

Suddenly, I focused on what CeeCee was saying.

And laughed.

"CeeCee," I said. "Are you nuts? Hang up the phone, go inside, and say yes."

"I should, shouldn't I? I just . . . I mean, I've been wanting this to happen for so long, and now it is, and I . . .well, I just can't believe it. . . ."

"CeeCee."

"Hanging up now," CeeCee said. And the line clicked.

He and Kelly had looked pretty . . . *friendly* on that couch. Maybe he'd given up. Maybe he was over the whole "us" thing.

Maybe now my life would go back to normal.

Maybe . . .

chapter *twelve*

"This is by the same director who made *Jaws*?" Jesse wanted to know. "I don't believe it."

Saturday night. Date night.

And, okay, though technically Jesse and I can't exactly go out (how could we, really?), Jesse does come over most Saturday nights. True, it isn't as romantic as dinner and a movie. And true, we have to be really quiet, so my family won't suspect I'm not alone in my room.

But at least we get to be together.

And yeah, on this particular Saturday night, I had a lot on my mind, none of which I had any intention of mentioning to Jesse.

But that didn't mean we couldn't spend a couple of hours watching videos. Jesse has a lot of catching up to do, movie-wise, considering the fact that they hadn't even been invented back when he'd been alive.

His favorite so far is *The Godfather*. I was hoping to cure him of this weakness by showing him *E.T.* How could anyone prefer Don Corleone over a six-year-old Drew Barrymore?

But Drew barely managed to hold Jesse's attention.

"*Jaws* is much better than this," Jesse said.

Jaws is another one of Jesse's favorites. He doesn't even like the right parts, either. He likes the part where all the men are showing one another their scars. Don't ask me why. I guess it's a guy thing.

Finally, I turned *E.T.* off and went, "Let's just talk."

By which, of course, I meant "Let's make out."

Which was working out very nicely until Jesse quit kissing me at one point and said, "I almost forgot. What was Paul doing at the Mission tonight? Has he found religion?"

This was so outlandish that I pulled my arms from around his neck and went, "*What?*"

"Your friend Paul," Jesse said. I may have let go of him, but he wasn't letting go of me. While this was nice, it was also just a little distracting. Especially the way his lips were still moving along mine. "I saw him a little while ago in the basilica . . . which was closed, you know. Why would he be there after hours, do you think? He hardly seems the type to be considering a career in the priesthood. Unless he suddenly received his calling. . . ."

I wrenched myself away from him.

Well, if you'd suddenly been seized by stark white terror, you'd have done the same thing.

"Susannah?" Jesse stared at me, concern filling his dark brown eyes where just a few seconds earlier there'd been . . .

140

well, not concern. "Are you all right?"

"Oh, God." How could I have been so stupid? How, how, *how*? Here I was, watching movies—*movies*—with my boyfriend, never suspecting a thing. Thinking Paul would have to come here to the house if he wanted to travel back to Jesse's time. Thinking he wouldn't be able to go back if he didn't. Thinking he wouldn't dream of going back tonight, with his grandfather in the hospital. Thinking he and Kelly were together now, so why would he bother?

Paul didn't care about his grandfather. He didn't care about anyone in his family and never had.

And he certainly didn't care about Kelly. Why should he? Kelly didn't understand him, Kelly didn't know what he really was. . . .

And, of course, there was another landmark in this century that had existed in Jesse's as well. A place Felix Diego had probably gone often, during his day.

The Mission. The Junipero Serra Mission, which had been built back in the 1700s.

"I have to go," I said, stumbling to my feet and diving for my jacket. I felt sick to my stomach. "I'm sorry, Jesse, but I have to—"

"Susannah." Jesse was on his feet as well, taking hold of my arm in a grip that was as strong as it was gentle. Jesse would never hurt me. On purpose. "What is it? What is this about? Why do you care if Paul is in the basilica?"

"You don't understand," I said. I really did think I was going to be sick. I really did. It must have shown on my face because Jesse's grip on my arm suddenly got a good deal tighter . . .

. . . just as the expression his face got a lot grimmer.

"Try me, *querida*," he said in a voice that was as hard as his grasp.

And then—don't ask me how or what I was thinking because, truthfully, I don't think I was—it all came spilling out.

I hadn't wanted to tell him. Not because I didn't want to upset him. God, nothing like that. No, I didn't want him to find out for the most selfish of all reasons: I hadn't wanted to tell him for fear he'd agree with Father Dominic and my dad—that he'd prefer another chance at life than eternity as a ghost.

But out it poured, everything, from what Dr. Slaski had told me to what Father Dom had said on the phone just a few hours ago. It was a raging flood that couldn't be stopped, the torrent of words coming from my mouth. I wanted to stuff them back as quickly as they spilled out.

But it was too late. It was way too late.

Jesse listened unflinchingly, not interrupting me, even when I told him the part about my deal with Paul: our secret arrangement in which I endured Wednesday afternoon "mediator lessons" with him in exchange for his not sending my boyfriend to the netherworld.

"Only now he doesn't want to kill you, Jesse," I told him bitterly. "He wants to *save* you, save your life. He's going back through time to stop Felix Diego from killing you. And if he does that . . . if he does that . . . "

"You and I will never meet." Jesse's expression was calm, his voice its normal deepness.

Never had any statement sounded as chilling to me. It felt like a stab wound to the heart.

"Yes," I said frantically. "Can't you see, I've got to go down there—now. Right now—and stop him."

"No, *querida*," Jesse said, still in that unhurried voice. "You can't do that."

For a second, the terror that was gripping my heart seemed to squeeze it until it stopped. I thought I would die, right there on the spot.

Jesse wanted to live. My dad, Father Dominic, Dr. Slaski, Paul . . . they had been right. They had all been right, and *I* was the wrong one, *me*. Jesse would prefer to live than to have met me, to have known me . . .

. . . to have loved me. . . .

I should have known, of course. And I think deep down, I *did* know. What kind of person—especially one who'd died the age Jesse had been, just twenty—wouldn't want a chance to go back and live again, if he could? What kind of person wouldn't be willing to give up everything he had for that chance?

And what did Jesse have? Nothing. Nothing at all. Just me.

My dad had accused me long ago of being the thing that was holding Jesse back, keeping him from moving on. Father Dominic had said it, as well . . . that if I really loved him, I'd set him free.

And now I knew. Jesse himself would rather be free than be with me.

God. I'd been such a fool. Such a total fool.

Then Jesse let go of my arm.

But instead of saying what I'd expected him to—*You can't go after him, because I want the chance. I want the chance to live again, if I can*—he said in a voice gone suddenly as cold as the wind outside, "You can't go after him. He's too dangerous. I'll go. I'll stop him."

I wasn't sure I'd heard him right. Had he said—could he possibly have said—what I thought he'd said?

"Jesse," I said. "I don't think you understand. He wants to save you. To keep you from . . . from dying that night."

"I understand," Jesse said. "I understand that Paul is a fool who thinks he's God. I don't know what makes him think it's his right to play with my destiny. But I do know he's not going to succeed. Not if I can stop him."

My circulation seemed to spring to life. Suddenly, I could breathe again. Relief washed over me in waves.

He wanted to stay. Jesse wanted to stay. He would rather stay than live. *He would rather stay*—with me—*than live.*

"You can't," I said, my voice sounding freakishly high-pitched even to my own ears. That was the relief I felt, making me giddy. "You can't stop him, Jesse. Paul will—"

"And just what do *you* intend to do, Susannah?" he demanded sharply. And if I hadn't been convinced before of the sincerity of his wish to remain in this place and time, his gruff tone then would have been enough. "*Talk* him out of what he plans? No. It's too dangerous."

But love had given me courage I'd never even known I had. I shrugged into my leather motorcycle jacket and said, "Paul won't hurt me, Jesse. I'm the reason he's doing this, remember?"

"I don't mean Paul," Jesse said. "I mean time traveling. Slaski says it's dangerous?"

"Yes, but—"

"Then you're not doing it."

"Jesse, I'm not afraid—"

"No," Jesse said. There was a look in his eye I had never seen before. "I'm going. You're staying here. Leave everything to me."

"Jesse, don't be—"

But a second later, I saw that I was talking to thin air.

Because Jesse was gone.

I knew where he'd disappeared to, of course. He'd gone to the basilica, to have a word with Paul.

And I was betting that that word would be accompanied by a fist.

I was also betting Jesse was going to be too late. Paul wouldn't be at the Mission anymore by the time Jesse got to him.

Or rather, he would be. But not the basilica as we knew it.

There was only one thing, really, that I could do then. And that wasn't, as Jesse had urged, to leave everything to him. How could I, when I could quite possibly wake up in the morning with no memory of Jesse whatsoever?

I knew what I had to do.

And this time, I wasn't going to make the mistake of consulting with anybody beforehand.

I strode across the room, lifted my pillow, and pulled out the miniature portrait of Jesse—the one he'd given to his one-time fiancée, Maria. The one that I'd been sleeping on since the day I'd stolen—er—been given it.

Looking down into Jesse's dark, confident gaze, I closed my eyes and pictured him . . . pictured Jesse in this very room, only not looking as it did now, with a frilly canopy bed and princess phone (thanks, Mom).

No, instead I pictured it as it must have looked 150 years earlier. No ruffled white curtains over the bay window. No window seat scattered with fluffy pillows. No carpet over the wood floor. No—ack!—bathroom, but maybe one of those, what were they called? Oh yeah, chamber pots.

No cars. No cell phones. No computers. No microwaves. No refrigerators. No televisions. No stereos. No airplanes. No penicillin.

Just grass. Grass and trees and sky and wooden wagons and horses and dirt and . . .

And I opened my eyes.

And I was there.

chapter *thirteen*

It was my room, but it wasn't.

Where the canopy had stood sat a bed with a brass stand. The bed was covered with a brightly colored quilt, the kind of quilt that my mom would have gone nuts over if she'd seen it in some craft shop. Instead of my vanity table with its big light-up mirror, there was a chest of drawers with a pitcher and bowl on it.

There was no mirror anywhere, but on the floor was a rug woven from . . . well, lots of different stuff. It was kind of hard to see really well, because the only light was what little moonlight spilled in from the bay windows. There was no electric switch. I felt for it instinctively the minute I opened my eyes to so much darkness. Where the light switch had been was just wood.

Which could only have meant one thing.

I'd done it.

Whoa.

But where was Jesse? This room was empty. The bed didn't look as if it had been slept in anytime recently.

Had I come too late? Was Jesse already dead? Or had I come too early and Jesse hadn't yet arrived?

There was only one way to find out. I laid my hand on the doorknob—only, of course, there was no knob now, but a latch instead—and went out into the hallway.

It was nearly pitch-black in the hallway. There was no electric switch here, either. Instead, when I groped for it, my hand touched a framed picture, or something . . .

. . . that promptly fell off the wall with a banging sound, although no glass broke. I didn't know what to do. I couldn't find the thing I'd knocked over, it was too dark. So I continued down the stairs, navigating the various twists and turns by memory alone, since I had no light to guide me.

I saw the glow before I heard the quick footsteps approaching the bottom of the stairs. Someone was coming . . . someone holding a candle.

Jesse? Could it possibly be?

But when I reached the bottom of the stairs, I saw that it was a woman who was coming toward me, a woman holding not a candle but some kind of lantern. At first, I thought she must be enormously fat, and I was like, God, what could she have been eating? It's not like they had Twinkies back in Jesse's day . . . er, now, I mean.

But then I saw that she was wearing some sort of a hoopskirt, and that what I'd taken for girth was really just her clothes.

"Mary, Mother of God," the woman cried when she saw

me. "Where did you come from?"

I thought it better to ignore that question. Instead, I asked her as politely as I could, "Is Jesse de Silva here?"

"What?" The woman held the lantern higher and really peered at me. "Faith," she cried. "But you're a girl!"

"Um," I said. I would have thought this was obvious. My hair, after all, is pretty long, and I always wear it down. Plus, as always, I had on mascara. "Yes, ma'am. Is Jesse here? Because I really have to speak to him."

But the woman, instead of appreciating my politeness, pressed her lips together very firmly. Next thing I knew, she was reaching for the door, holding it open, and trying to shoo me through it.

"Out," she said. "Out with you, then. You should know we don't allow the likes of you in here. This is a respectable house, this is."

I just stood there gaping at her. A respectable house? Of course it was. It was MY house.

"I don't mean to cause trouble, ma'am," I said, since I could see how it would be a little weird to find a strange girl wandering around your house . . . even if it was a boarding-house. That happened to belong to me. Or at least to my mother and her new husband. "But I really need to speak to Jesse de Silva. Can you tell me if he—"

"What kind of fool do you take me for?" the woman demanded not very nicely. "Mr. de Silva wouldn't give the time of day to a . . . creature like you. Need to speak to Jesse de Silva, indeed! Out! Out of my house!"

And then, with a strength surprising for a woman in a

hoopskirt, she grabbed me by the collar of my leather motorcycle jacket, and propelled me out the door.

"Good riddance to bad rubbish," the woman said and slammed the door in my face.

Not just any door, either. My *own* door. My *own* front door, to *my* house.

I couldn't believe it. From what I'd been led to believe, from Jesse and those *Little House on the Prairie* books, things back in the 1800s had been all butter churns and reading out loud around the fire. Nothing about mean ladies throwing girls out of their own houses.

Chagrined, I turned around and started down the steps from the front porch . . .

. . . and nearly fell on my face. Because the steps weren't where they used to be. Or would be one day, I mean. And except for the moonlight, which was sadly lacking just then, due to a passing cloud, there was no light whatsoever to see by. I mean it, it was spookily dark. There was no reassuring glow of streetlights—I wasn't even sure there *was* a street where Pine Crest Drive ought to have been.

And, turning my head, I could see no lights on in any nearby windows . . . for all I could tell, there *were* no nearby windows. The house I was standing in front of might have been the only house for miles and miles. . . .

And I'd just been thrown out of it. I was stranded in the year 1850 with no place to go and no way to get there. Except, I guess, the old-fashioned way.

I could, I supposed, have walked to the Mission. That's where Paul had supposedly gone. I craned my neck, looking for the familiar red dome of the basilica, just visible from my front porch, perched as it was in the Carmel Hills.

But instead of seeing Carmel Valley stretched out below me, all winking lights stretching to the vast darkness of the sea, all I saw was dark. No lights. No red dome, lit up for the tourists. Nothing.

Because, I realized, there *were* no lights. They hadn't been invented yet. At least, not lightbulbs.

God. How could anybody find their way anywhere? What did they use to guide them, freaking stars?

I looked up to check out the star situation, wondering if it would help me, and nearly fell off the porch again. Because there were more stars in the sky than I had ever seen before in my life. The Milky Way was like a white streak in the sky, so bright it almost put the moon, finally flitting out from behind some clouds, to shame.

Whoa. No wonder Jesse was unimpressed whenever I successfully located the Big Dipper.

I sighed. Well, there was nothing else I could do, I supposed, but start hoofing it in the general direction of the Mission, and hope I ran into Paul—or Jesse . . . Past Jesse, I mean—on the way.

I had just found my way off the porch—down a set of rickety wooden steps, unlike the cement ones in place there now . . . I mean, in the present . . . *my* present—when it hit me. The first heavy, cold drops of rain.

Rain. I'm not kidding. No sooner had I looked up to see if it was really rain, or someone dumping their chamber pot out on me (*ew*) from the second floor than I saw the bank of big black clouds rolling in from the sea. I had been so distracted by all the stars, I hadn't noticed them before.

Great. I travel more than a century and a half through time, and what do I get for my efforts? Getting thrown out of my own house, and rain. A lot of it.

Lightning flashed, high up in the sky. A few seconds later, thunder rumbled, long and low.

Fabulous. A thunderstorm. I was stuck in an 1850 thunderstorm with nowhere to go.

Then the wind picked up, carrying with it a scent I couldn't place right away. It took me a minute to remember it. Then, all at once, I did: my occasional forays into Central Park back when I'd lived in Brooklyn.

Horse. There were horses nearby.

Which meant there had to be a barn. Which might be dry. And which might be unguarded by hoopskirted women who consider me bad rubbish.

Ducking my head against the rain, which was coming down harder now, I ran in the direction of the horse smell and soon found myself behind the house, facing an enormous barn, right where Andy had said he was going to have a pool installed one day, after we'd all finished college and he could afford it.

The barn doors were closed. I hurried toward them, praying they wouldn't be locked. . . .

They weren't. I heaved one open and slipped inside just as another bolt of lightning streaked through the sky, and thunder sounded again, more loudly, this time.

Inside the barn it was dry, at least. Black as tar, but dry.

The horse smell was strong—I could hear them moving uneasily around in their stalls, startled by the thunder—but the smell of something else was stronger. Hay, I think it was. Not exactly being a country girl, I couldn't say for sure. But I thought the stuff that crunched and rolled a little beneath my boots might be hay.

Well, this was just great. I'd come to save my boyfriend's life—or rather, to keep someone else from saving it—and all I'd accomplished so far was to enrage his landlady.

Oh and I'd been rained on. And found a barn.

Perfect. Dr. Slaski hadn't been kidding when he'd warned me against time travel. It sure hadn't been any picnic so far.

And when, a second later, I'd reached up to wring some of the water from my hair and felt a heavy hand on my shoulder—

Well, I had definitely had enough of the mid-1800s.

Fortunately for me, a roll of thunder drowned out my scream. Otherwise, the landlady—or worse, her husband, if she had one—would have been out here in a flash. And I probably would have gotten a lot more than just a bad scare.

"Shut up!" Paul whispered. "Do you want to get us both shot?"

I whirled around. I could only dimly make out his figure there in the darkness. But it was enough to send my pulse, which had been racing before, to a near standstill.

"What are you doing here?" I demanded, hoping he couldn't hear the confusion in my voice. I was feeling an odd mix of emotions at seeing him: anger, that he'd gotten there before me; fear, that he was there at all; and relief, at seeing a familiar face.

"What do you *think* I'm doing here?" Paul tossed something rough and heavy at me.

I caught it inexpertly. "What's this?"

"A blanket. So you can dry yourself off."

I gratefully threw the blanket around my shoulders. Even though I still had my motorcycle jacket on, I was shivering beneath the leather. I don't think it was from the rain, either.

The blanket smelled strongly of horse. But not in a bad way. I guess.

"So," Paul said and moved into the sliver of light thrown through the still-open barn door, so that I could finally see his face. "You made it."

I sniffled miserably. I tried not to pay attention to the fact that I was cold, wet, and inside a barn. In the year 1850.

"I can't believe you really thought you would get away with it," I said, glad I'd finally seemed to get the trembling of my voice under control. My chattering teeth were another story. "Did you think I wouldn't try to stop you?"

Paul shrugged. "I figured it was worth a try. And there's still a chance I'll succeed, you know, Suze. He isn't here yet."

"Who isn't?" I asked stupidly. I was still busy trying to figure out how I could possibly ditch Paul and get to Jesse without him noticing.

"Jesse," Paul said as if I were mentally impaired. And you know what? Probably I am. "We're a day early. He gets here tomorrow."

"How do you know?" I asked, wiping my dripping nose on the back of my wrist.

"I talked to that lady," he said. "Mrs. O'Neil. The one who owns your house."

"She talked to you?" I couldn't hide my surprise. "She wouldn't talk to me. She threw me out."

"What'd you do, materialize in front of her?" Paul asked with a sneer.

"No," I said. "Well, not *right* in front of her."

Paul shook his head. But I could see that he was grinning a little. "Bet you gave her a coronary. What'd she think of your getup?" He gestured at my clothes.

I looked down at myself. In my jeans and motorcycle jacket, I guess I didn't really resemble any nineteenth-century miss I'd ever seen in the movies. Or, more important, in pictures from the era.

"She said she ran a respectable house and I should know better than to show my face there," I admitted and was stung when Paul laughed out loud.

"What?" I demanded.

"Nothing," Paul said. But he was still laughing.

"Just tell me."

"Okay. But don't get mad. She thought you were a lady of the evening."

I glared at him. "She did not!"

"She did so. And I told you not to get mad."

155

"I'm not exactly dressed like a hoochie mama," I pointed out. "I'm wearing *pants*."

"That's the problem," Paul said. "No respectable woman in this century wears pants. Good thing Jesse didn't see you. He probably wouldn't even have talked to you."

I had had about all I could take of Paul. I said hotly, "He would so. Jesse's not like that."

"Not the Jesse you know," Paul said. "But we're not talking about the one you know, are we? We're talking about the one who's never met you. Who hasn't sat around for a hundred and fifty years, watching the world go by. We're talking about the Jesse who's on his way to Carmel to marry the girl of his—"

"Shut up," I said before he could finish that sentence.

Paul's grin got broader. "Sorry. Well, we've got a while to wait. No sense spending it arguing. Come up to the loft with me, and we'll sit out this storm together."

He slipped back into the shadows, and I heard a foot scrape on a wooden rung. One of the horses whinnied.

"Don't be scared, Suze," Paul called down to me from a few feet in the air. "They're just horses. They won't bite. If you don't get too near them."

That wasn't why I was scared. Not that I was about to admit any such thing to him.

"I think I'll stay down here," I said into the darkness his voice had come from.

"Fine by me," Paul said, "if you want to get caught. It'll just make my job easier. Mr. O'Neil came by a little while ago to check on the horses. I'm sure he wouldn't shoot a girl, though. If he realized you were a girl in time, I mean."

This got me moving toward the ladder.

"I hate you," I commented, as I started to climb.

"No, you don't," Paul said from the darkness above me. I could tell by his voice that he was grinning again. "But you go right on telling yourself that, if it makes you feel better."

chapter fourteen

It was warm in the loft. Warm and dry. And not just because of all the hay. No, also because Paul and I were sitting so close together—for body-heat purposes only, I'd informed him, when he'd shown me the hole he'd dug in the giant pile of hay at one end of the loft.

"Because I don't want to die of hypothermia," was what I'd said, since the horse blanket didn't seem to be doing the job. At least, my teeth hadn't stopped chattering. My jeans weren't drying as fast as I'd have liked them to.

"I'll keep my hands to myself," Paul had assured me.

And so far, he'd been true to his word.

"What I don't get," I said as the rain pelted down outside, with occasional flashes of lightning, though the thunderstorm portion of the evening seemed to be mostly over, "is what you're doing here. Aren't you supposed to be looking for Felix Diego? To stop him?"

"Yeah." In the darkness of the loft, I could only make out

Paul's profile by the light that crept in from chinks and knotholes in the wood that made up the barn walls.

"So . . . why aren't you? Unless"—my blood ran cold—"you already found him. But then why—"

"Relax, Simon," Paul said. "I didn't find him. Yet. But we both know he's due to show up here tomorrow, same as Jesse."

I did relax then. Well, just a little. So Paul hadn't gotten to Diego yet. Which meant there was still time . . .

To do what, though? What was I going to do when I found Jesse? I couldn't tell him not to stay at Mrs. O'Neil's boardinghouse or he'd be killed, because the truth was, I *wanted* him to be killed. How else was I ever going to get to meet him—okay, date him—in the twenty-first century?

I was just going to have to stick to Paul, was all. Stick to Paul and keep him from stopping Diego. Maybe I wouldn't even see Jesse. Which would probably be just as well. Because if I did, what on earth was I going to say to him? What if he, like Mrs. O'Neil, mistook me for some random hoochie mama? I didn't think I could bear it. . . .

Which reminded me . . .

"Are people going to notice we're gone?" I asked. "In our own time, I mean? Or when we get back, will it be like no time has gone by?"

"I don't know." I got the feeling Paul had been trying to get some sleep when I'd shown up. He seemed to be attempting to get back to it now and my endless questions were only serving to irritate him. "Why didn't you ask my grandfather? You two are so close and all. . . ."

"I didn't exactly get a chance, now, did I?" I stared at him—or tried to, anyway—in the darkness. I still wasn't sure why Dr. Slaski had chosen me as his confidante and not his own grandson. Well, except for the fact that Paul is a user. And a thief. And, oh yeah, had possibly purposefully drugged him.

"He's not who you think he is, Paul," I said, meaning Dr. Slaski. "He's not your enemy. He's just like us."

"Don't say that." Paul's blue-eyed gaze suddenly bore into me from the darkness. "Don't ever."

"Why? He's a mediator, Paul. A shifter. He's probably who you got it from. He knows a lot. And one thing he knows is that the more we play around with . . . with our powers . . . the better our chances of ending up like him—"

"I told you not to say that," Paul snapped.

"But if you'd just give him a chance, instead of calling him a gork and purposefully—"

"We're not like him, all right? You and I? We're nothing like him. He was stupid. He tried to tell people. He tried to tell people that mediators—shifters—whatever—that we exist. And everyone laughed at him. My dad had to change his name, Suze, because no one would take him seriously, knowing he was related to someone they all said was a quack. So don't you ever—*ever*—say we're like him or that we're going to end up like him. I already know how I'm going to end up."

I just blinked at him. "Oh, really? And how's that?"

"Not like him," Paul assured me. "I'm going to be like my dad."

"Your dad isn't a mediator," I reminded him.

"I mean I'm going to be rich, like my dad," Paul said.

"How?" I asked with a laugh. "By stealing from the people you're supposed to be helping?"

"There you go again," Paul said, shaking his head. "Who told you we're supposed to help the dead, Suze? Huh? Who?"

"You know perfectly well it was wrong of you to take that money. It wasn't yours."

"Yeah," Paul said. "Well, there's more where it came from and, unlike you, I suffer no moral compunctions in taking it. I'm going to be rich someday, Suze. And, unlike Grandpa Gork, in control."

"Not if you kill all your brain cells flitting in and out of the past," I pointed out.

"Yeah, well," Paul said. "This is a one-time trip. After this, I shouldn't need to go back again."

I stared at his profile. Only our sides were touching beneath the horse blanket we shared. Still, Paul radiated a lot of heat. I was getting a little hot under the blanket.

That was when I realized the only other guy I'd ever lain this close to was Jesse, and that the heat he gave off? Yeah, a lot of that was in my mind. Because ghosts can't give off heat. Even to mediators. Even to mediators who happen to be in love with them.

"It's wrong," I said quietly to Paul as I looked at his closed eyelids. "What you're doing to Jesse. He doesn't want it."

Paul's eyes opened at that.

"You *told* him?"

"He heard us talking about it," I said. "And he doesn't want it. He doesn't want you to interfere, Paul. He was going down to the Mission to stop you when I left."

Paul looked at me for a few seconds, his blue eyes unreadable in the darkness.

"Are you sleeping with him?" he asked bluntly.

I gaped at him, feeling heat flood my cheeks. "Of course not!" Then, realizing what I'd said, stammered, "N-not that it's any of your business."

But Paul, rather than grinning over his so fully discomfiting me, as I would have expected him to, was gazing down at me very seriously.

"Then I don't get it," he said simply. "Why him? Why not me?"

Oh. *That.*

"Because he's honest," I said. "And he's kind. And he puts me ahead of everything else—"

"So would I," Paul said. "If you'd give me the chance."

"Paul," I said. "If we were in an earthquake or something, and you had a chance to save me but it was at the risk of your own life, you would save yourself, not me."

"I would not! How can even you say that?"

"Because it's true."

"But you're saying that your perfect Jesse would save you, at the risk of his own life?"

"Yes," I said with absolute certainty. "Because he has. In the past."

"No, he hasn't, Suze," Paul said with equal certainty.

"Yes, he has, Paul. You don't even know—"

"Yes, I do know. Jesse could never possibly have risked his own life to save yours, because in all the time you've known him, he's been dead. So he hasn't been risking anything, all those times he's saved you. Has he?"

I opened my mouth to deny to this, then realized that Paul was right. It was the truth. A screwed-up version of the truth, but the truth just the same.

"What have you got to be so bitter about?" I demanded instead. "You've always gotten everything you've ever wanted your whole life. You've only had to ask for it, and it was yours. But it's like it's never enough for you."

"I haven't gotten *everything* I've ever wanted," Paul said pointedly. "Although I'm working to correct that."

I shook my head, knowing what he meant.

"You only want me because you can't have me, Paul," I said. "And you know it. I mean, my God. You've got Kelly. All the guys in school want her."

"All the guys in school," Paul said, "are idiots."

I ignored that.

"You would be a lot better off," I said, "if you'd just be happy with what you have, Paul, instead of wanting what you'll never get."

But Paul kept right on grinning. Grinning and rolling back over so he could sleep. "I wouldn't be so sure of that, if I were you, Suze," he said in a tone that sounded way too smug to me.

"You—"

"Go to sleep, Suze," Paul said.

"But you—"

"We've got a long day ahead of us. Just sleep."

Amazingly, I did. Sleep, I mean. I hadn't expected that I'd be able to. But maybe Dr. Slaski was right. Traveling through time DOES wear you out. I don't think I'd have fallen asleep otherwise . . . you know, given the hay, the horses, the rain, and, oh yeah, the hot-but-totally-deadly guy lying next to me.

But I laid my head down, and next thing I knew, lights-out.

I woke with a start. I hadn't even realized I'd been asleep. But there was light streaming through the slits between the wood planks that made up the sides of the barn. Not the gray light of dawn, either. It was full-on sunlight, revealing that I'd slept way past 8:00. . . .

And kneeling in front of me was Paul, with breakfast.

"Where'd you get *that*?" I asked, sitting up. Because in Paul's hands was a pie. A whole pie. Apple, from the smell of it.

And it was still warm.

"Don't ask," he said, pulling, of all things, two forks from his back pocket. "Just eat."

"Paul." I could hear movement below. Paul had been speaking in hushed tones. I knew why now.

We were not alone.

A man's voice said, "Git along there." He appeared to speaking to the horses.

"Did you steal this?" I asked, even as I was taking the fork and digging in. Time travel doesn't just make you sleepy. It makes you hungry, too.

"I told you not to ask," Paul said as he, too, shoveled a forkful of pie into his mouth,

Stolen or not, it was good. Not the best I'd ever had, by any means—I don't know if, out in the Wild West, they really had access to the best sugar and stuff.

But it satisfied the rumbling in my stomach . . . and soon made me aware of another urge.

Paul seemed to read my mind.

"There's an outhouse behind the barn," he informed me.

"A *what* house?"

"You know." Paul grinned. "Watch out for the spiders."

I thought he was joking.

He wasn't. There were spiders. Worse, what they had to use as toilet paper back then? Let's just say that today, it wouldn't be considered fit to *write on*, let alone . . . you know . . . anything else.

Plus I had to hurry, so no one would see me in my twenty-first-century clothes and ask questions.

But it was hard because once I'd slipped out of the barn, I was flabbergasted by what I saw. . . .

Which was nothing.

Really. Nothing, in all directions. No houses. No telephone poles. No paved roads. No Circle K. No In-N-Out Burger. Nothing. Just trees. And a dirt track that I suppose passed for a street.

I could, however, see the red dome of the basilica. There it was, down in the valley below us, with the sea behind it. That, at least, hadn't changed in the last 150 years.

Thank God plumbing has, however.

When I crept back up to the loft, there was no sign of Mr. O'Neil. He appeared to have taken his horses and gone off to do whatever it was men like him did all day in 1850. Paul was waiting for me with an odd look on his face.

"What?" I asked, thinking he was going to tease me about the outhouse.

"Nothing," was all he said, however. "Just . . . I have a surprise for you."

Thinking it was another food-related item, although I was quite full from the pie, I said, "What? And don't tell me it's an Egg McMuffin, because I know they don't have drive-through here."

"It's not," Paul said.

And then, moving faster than I'd ever seen him move before, he took something else from his back pocket—a length of rope. Then he grabbed me.

People have, of course, tied me up before. But never somebody whose tongue was once in my mouth. I really wasn't expecting Paul to do something so underhanded. Save my boyfriend's life so I'd never meet him, yes. But hog-tie my hands behind my back?

Not so much.

I struggled, of course. I got in a few good elbow jabs. But I couldn't scream, not if I didn't want Mrs. O'Neil to show up and go running for the sheriff or whatever. I wouldn't be able to help Jesse from jail.

But it appeared I wouldn't be much help to him for the time being, either.

"Believe me," Paul said as he tightened knots that were already practically cutting off my circulation. "This hurts me a lot more than it hurts you."

"It does not," I said, struggling. But it was hard to struggle when I was on my stomach in the hay, and his knee was in the small of my back.

"Well," he said, going to work on my feet now. "You're right, I guess. Actually, this doesn't hurt me at all. And it'll keep you out of trouble while I go find Diego."

"There's a special place for people like you, Paul," I informed him, spitting out hay. I was getting really sick of hay.

"Reform school?" he asked lightly.

"Hell," I informed him.

"Now, Suze, don't be that way." He finished with my feet and, just to be sure I wouldn't get it into my head to, I don't know, roll out of the hayloft, he tied one end of the rope to a nearby post. "I'll be back to untie you just as soon as I kill Felix Diego. Then we can go home."

"Where I'll never speak to you again," I informed him.

"Sure you will," Paul said cheerfully. "You won't remember any of this. Because we won't have gone back through time to save Jesse. Because you won't even know who Jesse is."

"I hate you," I said, really meaning it this time.

"You do now," Paul agreed. "But you won't when you wake up tomorrow in your own bed. Because without Jesse, I'll be the best thing that ever happened to you. It'll just be you and me, two shifters against the world. Won't that be fun?"

"Why don't you go—"

But I didn't get to finish that sentence, because Paul took something else out of his pocket. A clean white handkerchief. He'd told me once that he always carried one because you never know when you might need to gag someone.

"Don't you dare!" I hissed at him.

But it was too late. He wadded the handkerchief into my mouth and secured it there with another piece of rope.

If I had never hated him before, I did then. Hated him with every bone in my body, every beat of my heart. Especially when he gave me a pat on the head and said, "See ya."

Then disappeared down the ladder to the barn floor.

chapter *fifteen*

I don't know how long I lay there like that. Long enough to start wondering whether I could just close my eyes and shift home. Who knew where I'd end up? Somewhere in the backyard, anyway. Possibly in a big bunch of poison oak, since there was no barn there now. But anything had to be better than lying in a very cramped position on the floor of a hayloft, with who knew what crawling through my hair and the blood pounding in my temples.

But a world without Jesse? Because that's what I'd be guaranteeing myself if I gave up now. A world without my one purpose for living. Well, more or less. I mean, I know women need men like fish need bicycles, and all of that. Except . . .

Except I love him.

I couldn't do it. I was too selfish. I wasn't going to give up. Not yet. There were still plenty of hours of daylight left, or at least, there had been when Paul had left. The shadows,

I couldn't help noticing, were growing longer.

Still, if Mrs. O'Neil had told Paul the truth, and Jesse was expected that night, there was still time. Paul might not find Diego. He might have to come back with his task unaccomplished. And when he did, and he untied me . . .

Well, he was going to learn a lot about pain, that was for sure. Because this time, I'd be ready for him.

I don't know how much time passed while I lay there, plotting my revenge on Paul Slater. Death was too good for him, of course. An eternity as a ghost—floating shiftlessly through this dimension and the next—was what would suit him best. Give him a little taste of what it had been like for Jesse all of these years. That ought to teach him. . . .

I could do it, too. I could pull Paul's soul out of his body and make it so that he could never return to it . . .

. . . by giving that body to someone else. Someone who deserved a chance to live again. . . .

But I couldn't. I knew I couldn't. I couldn't kiss Paul's lips, even if I knew it was Jesse inside them, kissing me back. It was just too . . . gross.

It was as I was lying there thinking this that I heard it, a sound my ears had become so finely attuned to over the past year that I could have been at the Super Bowl, a million rows away, and I still would have heard it.

Jesse's voice.

He was calling to someone. I couldn't hear what, exactly, he was saying. But he sounded, I don't know. Different, somehow.

He was getting closer, too. His voice, I mean.

He was coming toward the barn.

He'd found me. I don't know how—Dr. Slaski hadn't said anything about ghosts being able to travel through time. But maybe they could. Maybe they could, just like shifters, and Jesse had done it, he'd come back through time looking for me. To save me. To help me save him.

I closed my eyes, thinking his name as hard as I could. This worked, more often than not. Jesse would materialize in front of me, wondering what on earth was so urgent.

Only he didn't. Not this time. I opened my eyes, and . . . nothing.

Only I could still his voice below me. He was saying, "No, no, it's all right, Mrs. O'Neil."

Mrs. O'Neil. Mrs. O'Neil could see Jesse?

The barn door opened. I heard it creak. Then . . .

Footsteps.

But how could Jesse have footsteps? He's a ghost.

Wriggling as far toward the edge of the hayloft as I could, I craned my neck, trying to see what I could only hear. But the rope Paul had used to tie my feet to the post wouldn't let me wiggle more than a few feet from my original position. I could hear him now, though—really hear him. He was speaking in a soft, soothing tone to . . . to . . .

To his horse.

Jesse was talking to a horse. I heard it whinny softly in reply.

Which was when I finally knew. This wasn't Ghost Jesse, come to rescue me. This was Alive Jesse, who didn't even know me. Alive Jesse, come to meet his fate in my room tonight.

I froze, feeling pins and needles all over—and not just because I'd been lying in such a cramped position for so long. I needed to see him. I *needed* to see him. Only how?

Then he moved and I turned my head, following the sound . . .

. . . and saw, through a chink in the floorboards of the loft, a spot of color. His horse. It was his horse. I saw his hands moving over the saddle, unstrapping it. It was Jesse. He was right beneath me. He was—

Why I did what I did next, I'll never know. I didn't want Jesse to know I was there. If Jesse found me, it could throw off everything. Who knew, he might not even be murdered that night. And then I'd never get to meet him.

But the urge to see him—alive—was so strong, that without even thinking about it, I banged my feet as hard as I could on the hayloft floor.

The hands moving over the saddle grew suddenly still. He'd heard me. I tried to call to him, but all that came out, thanks to Paul's gag, was *gnnh, gnnh.*

I banged my feet harder.

"Is someone there?" I heard Jesse call.

I banged again.

This time, he didn't call out. He started climbing the ladder to the loft. I heard the wood strain beneath his weight.

His weight. Jesse had *weight.*

And then I saw his hands—his large, brown, capable hands—on the top rung of the ladder, followed, a second later, by his head. . . .

The breath froze in my lungs.

Because it was him. It was Jesse.

But not Jesse as I'd ever seen him before. Because he was alive. He was . . . *there.* He was so solidly and unquestionably *there*, taking up space like he *owned* it, like the space better get out of *his* way, as opposed to the other way around.

He wasn't glowing. He was radiating. Not the spectral glow I was used to seeing around him, either, but instead an undeniable aura of health and vitality. It was like the Jesse I had known was a pale replica—a reflection—of the one I was looking at now. Never had I been so aware of the way his dark hair curled against the back of his tanned neck; the deep brown of his eyes; the whiteness of his teeth; the strength in those long legs as he knelt down beside me; the tendons in the back of his brown hands; the sinews in his bare arms. . . .

"Miss?"

And his voice. His voice! So deep, it seemed to reverberate down my spine. It was Jesse's voice all right, but suddenly, it was in surround sound, it was THX, it was . . .

"Miss? Are you all right?"

Jesse was gazing down at me, his dark eyes filled with concern. One of his hands moved to his boot, and the next thing I knew, a long and shiny blade was gleaming in his hand. I watched in fascination as the blade came nearer and nearer to my cheek.

"Don't be afraid," Jesse was saying. "I'm going to untie you. Who did this to you?"

Suddenly, the gag was gone. My mouth was raw from

where the rope had cut into it. Then my hands were free. Sore, but free.

"Can you speak?" Jesse's hands were on my feet now, his knife neatly slicing through the ropes Paul had tied me with. "Here."

He laid the knife aside and lifted something else toward my face. Water. From a flask. I took it from him and sucked greedily. I'd had no idea how thirsty I'd been.

"Easy," Jesse said in that voice—*that voice!* "I can get you more. Stay here and I'll get help—"

On the word *help*, however, my hands, as if of their own volition, dropped the flask and flew out to seize his shirt-front instead.

It wasn't the shirt I was used to seeing Jesse in. It was similar, the same soft, white linen. But this one was higher at the neck. He was wearing a vest, too—a waistcoat, I think they were called back then—of a sort of watered silk.

"No," I croaked and was startled at how raspy my voice sounded. "Don't go."

Not, of course, because I was worried he was going to go and get Mrs. O'Neil, who'd recognize me as the strumpet she'd found wandering around her front parlor the night before. But because I couldn't bear the thought of him leaving my sight. Not now. Not ever.

This was Jesse. This was the *real* Jesse. This was who I loved.

And who was going to die shortly.

"Who are you?" Jesse asked, lifting the flask I'd dropped and, finding it not quite empty, handing it back to me.

174

"Who did this—left you here like this?"

I drank what was left of the water. I'd known Jesse long enough to see that he was outraged—outraged at whoever had left me like that.

"A . . . a man," I said. Because, of course, Jesse—this Jesse—wouldn't know who Paul was. . . . Didn't know who I was, clearly.

His eyebrows furrowed, the one with the scar in it looking particularly adorable. The scar wasn't as obvious, I noticed, on Live Jesse as it was on Ghost Jesse.

"And did this same man put you in these outlandish clothes?" Jesse wanted to know, looking critically at my jeans and motorcycle jacket.

Suddenly, I wanted to laugh. He seemed like a different Jesse entirely—or rather, a hundred times more real than the Jesse I had known—but his disgust with my wardrobe? That hadn't changed a bit.

"Yes," I said. I figured it would be more believable to him than the real explanation.

"I'll see him horsewhipped," Jesse said as matter-of-factly as if he had people horsewhipped for dressing girls up in odd outfits and leaving them tied up in haylofts every day of the week. "Who are you? Your family must be looking for you—"

"Um," I said. "No, they aren't. I mean . . . I doubt it. And my name is Suze."

Again the dark brow furrowed. "Soose?"

"Suze," I said with a laugh. I couldn't help it. Laughing, I mean. It was so wonderful to see him like this. "Susannah.

As in 'Oh, Susannah, Don't You Cry for Me.'"

It was what I had said to him, I realized with a pang, back in my bedroom, the very first time I'd met him, the day I'd arrived in Carmel. I hadn't known then what I knew now—that that moment had been a turning point in my life—everything before it was BJ: Before Jesse. Everything afterward, AJ: After Jesse. I hadn't known then that this guy in the puffy shirt with the tight black pants would one day mean more to me than my own life . . . would one day be my everything.

But I knew it now, just as I knew something else:

I had it wrong. I had it all wrong.

But it wasn't, I knew, too late to fix it. Thank God.

"Susannah," Jesse said, as he sat beside me in the straw. "Susannah O'Neil, perhaps? You are related to Mr. and Mrs. O'Neil? Let me get them. I know they'll want to see that you're safe—"

"No," I said, shaking my head. "My, um, family is far away." *Really* far away. "You can't get them. I mean, thank you, but . . . you can't get them."

"Then this man . . ." Jesse looked excited. And why not? It probably wasn't every day the guy stumbled over a sixteen-year-old girl who'd been left bound and gagged in a hayloft. "Who is he? I'll fetch the sheriff. He must pay for what he's done."

Much as I would have liked to sic Jesse—Live Jesse—on Paul, it didn't seem like the appropriate thing to do. Not when Jesse was going to have so many problems of his own to handle very soon. Paul was my problem, not his.

"No," I said. "No, that's okay." Then, seeing his puzzled look, I said, "I mean, that's all right. Don't get the sheriff—"

"You needn't fear him anymore, Susannah," Jesse said gently. He clearly did not know he was speaking to a girl who had kicked a lot of butt in her day. Ghost butt, mostly, but whatever. "I won't let him hurt you again."

"I'm not afraid of him, Jesse," I said.

"Then—" Jesse's face clouded suddenly. "Wait. How did you know my name?"

Ah. Well, there was the rub, wasn't it?

Jesse was looking at me curiously, that dark-eyed gaze raking my face. I'm sure I must have looked a picture. I mean, what girl wouldn't after having been left for hours with her head in the straw and her mouth gagged?

It didn't matter, of course. What Jesse thought of me. But I felt self-conscious just the same. I reached up and shoved some hair out of my eyes, trying to tuck it back behind an ear. Just my luck, the first time I meet my boyfriend—while he's still living—and I look like a complete train wreck.

"Do I know you?" Jesse asked, his gaze searching. "Have we met? Are you . . . are you one of the Anderson girls?"

I had no idea who the Anderson girls might be, but I felt a stab of envy for them, whoever they were. Because they were girls who'd gotten to know Jesse—Live Jesse. I wondered if they knew how lucky they were.

"We haven't met," I said. "Yet. But . . . I know you. I mean, I know . . . about you."

"You do?" Recognition dawned at last in his gaze. "Wait

. . . yes! Now I know. You're friends with one of my sisters. From school? Mercedes? You know Mercedes?"

I shook my head, fumbling around in the pocket of my leather jacket.

"Josefina, then?" Jesse studied me some more. "You must be close to her age, fifteen, yes? You don't know Josefina? You can't know Marta, she's too old—"

I shook my head again, then held out what I'd fished from my pocket.

He looked down at what I held in my hand.

"*Nombre de Dios,*" he said softly, and took it from me.

It was the miniature portrait of Jesse, the one I'd stolen from the Carmel Historical Society. I saw now how poor a portrait it actually was. Oh, the painter had gotten the shape of Jesse's head right and his eye color and expression were close enough.

But he'd completely failed to capture what it was that made Jesse . . . well . . . Jesse. The keen intelligence in his dark brown eyes. The confident twist of his wide, sensuous mouth. The gentleness of his cool, strong hands. The power—just now leashed, but coiled so close to the surface, it might rise up at any moment—of those muscles, honed from years of working alongside his father's ranch hands, beneath that soft linen shirt and black pants.

"Where did you get this?" Jesse demanded, his fist closing over the portrait. Sparks seem to fly from his dark eyes, he was that angry. "Only one person has a portrait like this."

"I know," I said. "Your fiancée, Maria. You're here to marry her. Or at least, that's the plan. You're on your way to see her now, but her father's ranch is still pretty far off, so you're staying here for the night before you go on to her place in the morning."

Anger turned to bewilderment as Jesse lifted his free hand and raked his fingers through his thick dark hair—a gesture I had seen him perform so many times when he was completely frustrated with me, that tears actually sprang to my eyes, it was so familiar . . . and so adorable.

"How do you know all this?" he asked desperately. "You're . . . you're friends with Maria? Did she . . . give you this?"

"Not exactly," I said.

And took a deep breath.

"Jesse, my name is Susannah Simon," I said all in a rush, wanting to get it out before I changed my mind. "I'm what's called a mediator. I'm from the future. And I'm here to keep you from being murdered tonight."

chapter *sixteen*

Because, in the end, I couldn't do it.

I thought I could. I really did think I could sit back and let Jesse be murdered. I mean, if the alternative was never to meet him? Sure, I could do it. No problem.

But that had been before. Before I'd seen him. Before I'd spoken to him. Before he'd touched me. Before I'd known what he was, what he could have been, if he'd only lived.

I knew now I could no more stand by and let Jesse be killed than I could have . . . well, shoved my little stepbrother David out in front of a speeding car or fed my mother poison mushroom caps. I couldn't let Jesse die, even if meant never seeing him again. I loved him too much.

It was as simple as that.

Oh, I knew I was going to hate myself later. I knew I was going to wake up and, if I even remembered what I'd done, hate myself for the rest of my natural life.

But what else could I do? I couldn't stand idly by while someone I loved was walking into mortal danger. Father Dominic, my dad, all of them—even Paul—were right. I had to save Jesse if I could.

It was the right thing to do.

But not, of course, the easy thing. The easy thing would have been to point a finger in his face as he stared down at me, completely disbelieving, and gone, "Ha! Fooled ya! Just kidding."

Instead, I said, "Jesse. Did you hear me? I said I'm here from the future to save you from being—"

"I heard what you said." Jesse smiled at me gently. "Do you know what I think would be best? If you would let me get Mrs. O'Neil. She'll take good care of you while I go to town to get the doctor. Because I think the man who did this to you—tied you like this—might also have hit you on the head—"

"Jesse," I said flatly. I couldn't believe this. Here I was, making this tremendous sacrifice, saving the love of my life and knowing that I would never be with him again, and he was accusing me of being bonkers. "Paul didn't hit me in the head. All right? I'm fine. A little thirsty still, but otherwise fine. I just need you to listen to me. Tonight Felix Diego is going to sneak into your room here at the boardinghouse and strangle you to death. Then he's going to throw your body into a shallow grave, and no one is going to find it until a century and a half later, when my stepdad installs a hot tub on our deck."

Jesse just looked down at me. I couldn't be sure, but I

think I saw pity in his gaze.

"Jesse, I'm serious," I said. "You've got to go home. Okay? Just get back on your horse and turn around and go home, and don't even think about marrying Maria de Silva."

"Maria did send you," Jesse said, finally. His face darkened with a sudden anger. "This is her way of trying to save face, is it? Well, you can go back to your mistress and tell her it won't work. I won't have her family thinking I wasn't gentleman enough to break it off in person—no matter who she sends with strange tales to frighten me off. I'm going to see her tomorrow whether she likes it or not."

I blinked up at him, completely dumbfounded. What was he talking about?

Then, too late, I remembered the secret Jesse had once confided in me, the secret only I knew . . . that he had been on his way to the de Silva ranch all those years ago not to marry Maria, but to break things off with her . . .

. . . Which explained why all of her letters to him had been discovered alongside his remains last summer, when my stepbrother accidentally dug them up. Nineteenth-century manners demanded that couples breaking off their engagements returned the letters each had written the other. Diego had murdered Jesse before such an exchange could take place in order to prevent Maria's father from asking any uncomfortable questions concerning the break-up—like what Jesse had heard about his fiancée that had made him want to end their engagement.

"Wait," I said. "Hold on. Jesse, Maria didn't send me. I

don't even know Maria. Well, I mean, we've met, but—"

"You have to know her." Jesse looked down at the framed portrait in his hand. "She gave this to you. She must have. How else could you have gotten it?"

"Um," I said, with a shrug. "Actually, I stole it." Then I saw his face change, and knew I'd made a mistake.

"Oh, no," I said, holding up both hands, palms toward him. "Down, boy. I didn't steal it from your precious Maria, believe me. I stole it from the Carmel Historical Society, okay? A museum, where it had been sitting for God knows how long. In fact, I bet if you check with good old Maria, she still has hers. Her portrait of you, I mean."

"There were no duplicates made," Jesse said, in a hard voice.

"I know that." God, this was hard. "But look at the one you're holding, Jesse. Look how old it looks, how cracked the paint is, how tarnished that frame's gotten. That's because it's nearly two hundred years old. I stole it in the *future*, Jesse. I used it to help me get back here, to the past, so I could warn you . . ." This wasn't strictly true, of course, but close enough. "You've got to believe me, Jesse. Paul— the guy who tied me up—will back me up on this. He's out looking for Felix Diego right now to try to stop him before he can get to you—"

Jesse shook his head.

"I don't know who you are," he said in a low, even tone unlike any he'd ever used with me before. "But I'm returning this—" He dangled his portrait in my face. "—to its rightful owner. Whatever game you're playing, it ends *now*. Do you understand?

Game? I couldn't believe this. Here I was, risking my neck for him, and he was *mad* at me for stealing a stupid portrait of him? "There's no game, Jesse, okay? If this were just a game—if Maria really did send me—how would I know the stuff I know? How would I know that Maria and Diego are secretly in love? How would I know that your girl-friend—who is quite the skank, by the way—doesn't want to marry you at all? And that her dad doesn't approve of Diego and thinks if she marries you she'll forget about him even-tually? How do I know that the two of them have cooked up a scheme to kill you tonight and hide your body so it looks as though you skipped out on the engagement—"

"*Nombre de Dios.*" Jesse was on his feet and swearing. I couldn't help noticing how the loft shook a little under his footsteps. This was not something that would have hap-pened with Ghost Jesse, and was just more proof of how very far I'd come from the world I knew.

But that wasn't the only thing that wouldn't have hap-pened with Ghost Jesse. I realized this a second later when Alive Jesse bent down and siezed me by my arms, and gave me a frustrated shake.

"You know all this because Maria told you!" he said, from between gritted teeth. "Admit it! She told you!" As quickly as he'd snatched me up, he let go and turned away. Uttering a groan of pent-up annoyance, Jesse dragged a hand through his hair.

My arms, where he'd touched me, tingled.

"Look, I'm sorry," I said, meaning it. I knew how he felt,

after all. His wasn't the only heart in that barn that was breaking. "I mean, about your girlfriend wanting to kill you and all. Even if you were going to, you know, break up and all. But if it's any consolation, I do think you're a lot better off without her. I mean, the only times I ever met her, she was trying to kill me, too, but still. Better you find out she's a skank now, you know, and break it off cleanly, than find out after you're married. Because I don't even know if they let people get divorced in, you know, your time."

"Stop saying that!" Both of Jesse's hands went to grasp his hair now.

"What? Skank?" Maybe I *was* being a little harsh. "Well, okay. But the girl seems like major bad news."

"No." Jesse turned around to stare down at me, and I was surprised at the intensity with which his gaze burned into mine. *"Your time. The future.* You . . . you . . . I'm sorry, Miss Susannah. But I'm afraid I'm going to have to get the sheriff after all. Because you are very clearly not right in the head."

"Miss Susannah!" To my utter horror, tears prickcd at the corners of my eyes. But I couldn't help it. It was just so . . . so . . .

Unfair.

"So it's Miss Susannah, is it?" I asked him, ignoring my tears. "Oh, that's just great. I come all the way back here, risking major brain cell burnout, and you don't even believe me? I'm basically guaranteeing myself a lifetime of heart-break, and all you have to say is that you think I'm not right in the head? Thanks a lot, Jesse. No, really. That's just fine."

I broke off with a sob. Suddenly, it was all too much. I couldn't even look at him, because every time I did, he dazzled my eyes, like he was the most glorious Christmas tree that had ever existed. I buried my face in my hands and wept.

Maybe I had done enough, I told myself. Maybe tipping him off about Maria and Diego's plan would make him turn around tonight and go home. Even though the tip had come from what he obviously considered an unreliable source. I couldn't do anything more, could I? I mean, how else could I get him to believe me?

Then I remembered.

I dropped my hands from my face and looked up at him, not caring if he saw my tears.

"Doctor," I said.

"Yes." Jesse had fished a handkerchief from somewhere and handed it to me, his anger apparently dissipated. "Let me get one for you. I really feel that, despite what you say, Miss Susannah, you are unwell—"

"No." I pushed the handkerchief away impatiently. "Not for me. You."

A small smile appeared at the corners of his lips. "*I* need a doctor? I assure you, Miss Susannah, I have never felt fitter in my life."

"No." I stumbled to my feet. It was the first time I'd tried to stand since he'd untied me, and I wasn't exactly steady.

Still, I managed to get up without his help. Now I stood in front of him, breathing hard—but from emotion not exertion.

"A doctor," I said, looking up into his confident, concerned face. He was a good six inches taller than me, but I didn't care. I kept my chin up.

"You secretly want to be a doctor," I said. "You haven't asked him, but you know your father won't let you. He needs you to run the ranch, because you're the only boy. They couldn't spare you long enough for you to get through medical school, anyway."

Something happened to Jesse's face then. The glint of suspicion that I'd seen in his eye since I'd shown him the miniature portrait dropped away, and in its place came something else. . . .

Something like wonder.

"How . . . ?" Jesse stared down at me in utter incredulity. "How could you possibly have . . . ? I have never told anyone that."

I reached out and took one of his hands . . .

. . . and was shocked by how warm it felt in mine. All those times Jesse had held me . . . all those times he'd stroked my hair and I'd marveled at his heat . . . I knew now it hadn't been real, that heat. It had all been in my head. This, *this* heat was real. This hand was real. The hard calluses I knew so well . . . they were real. Really Jesse.

"You told me," I said to him. "You told me in the future."

Jesse shook his head, but not hard. Just a little.

"That . . . that's not possible," he said.

"Yes," I said. "Yes, it is. You see, what happens tonight is that Diego kills you. But only your body dies, Jesse. Your soul doesn't go anywhere, because . . . well, because I think it wasn't supposed to happen like that." I gazed up at him tenderly, still holding his hand. "I think you were supposed to live. But you didn't. So your soul hung around until I came along, about a hundred and fifty years later. I'm someone who helps . . . well, people who've died. You told me you wanted to be a doctor, Jesse. You told me in the future. Do you believe me now? Will you *please* go away from here and never come back?"

Jesse looked down at our entwined fingers, mine so pale against his sun-darkened skin, so soft against his calluses. He didn't say anything. What *could* he have said, really?

But because he was Jesse, he thought of something to say . . . the exact right thing to say.

"If you know something like that about me," he said softly, "about my wanting to be a doctor—something I have never told Maria—or any living person—then I must . . . I suppose I must . . . believe you."

"So," I said. "Now you know. You've got to get out of here, Jesse. Just get on your horse and ride."

"I will," he said.

We were standing so close, all he'd have had to do was reach out, and he could have cupped my face in his hand.

He didn't, of course.

But I could feel the warmth radiating from him, not just from the hand I held, but along the course of his entire body. He was so vibrant, so alive, that he made me feel aware of every hair on my head, every corpuscle in my skin. I loved him so much . . .

. . . and he'd never, ever know it.

But that was all right. Because at least he'd be able to go on living.

"But not," Jesse said, suddenly dropping my hand and turning away, "tonight."

I stood there, feeling as if I'd been kicked. Cool air rushed into all the places that, moments before, had been warmed by his body heat.

"W-what?" I stammered stupidly. "Not what?"

"Not tonight," Jesse said with a nod toward the barn doors, through which, I could see, the lengthening shadows were gone. The sun had set. There were no shadows anymore. "Tomorrow I will ride to the de Silvas' ranch to speak with Maria and her father. But not tonight. It's growing late. Too late to travel. I'll stay here tonight, and leave in the morning."

"But you can't!" The words were wrenched from the depths of my soul. "You've got to leave now, Jesse, tonight! You don't understand, it's too dangerous—"

An all-too-familiar smile crept across those lips I knew so well. "I can take care of myself, Miss Susannah," he said. "I am not afraid of Felix Diego."

I couldn't believe what was happening right before my eyes.

"Well, you should be!" I practically screamed. "Considering that he kills you!"

"Ah," Jesse said. "But if I understand you correctly, that was before you came to warn me . . . for which I thank you."

I couldn't believe how badly this was going.

"Jesse," I said, making one last desperate attempt to

reason with him. "You can't spend the night in that house. Do you understand? It's way, way too dangerous."

But Jesse surprised me. Well, why not? He always had.

"I understand," he said.

"You do?" I stared at him. "Really? Then you'll go?"

"No," he said, "I won't go."

"But—"

"I will stay here," he said, nodding to indicate the loft. "With you. Until morning."

I gaped at him.

"Here?" I echoed. "Here . . . in the barn?"

"With you," Jesse said.

"With me?"

"Yes," he said.

It took me until that moment to realize what he was doing. Here I was, traveling back 150 years to protect him—well, *now* that's what I was doing, anyway—and *he* was trying to protect *me*.

That was just so pure Jesse that I almost started to cry. Really.

But only almost.

Because his next question distracted me. "I have to ask, though. . . . Why?" His dark-eyed gaze raked my face.

"Why what?" I murmured, hypnotized as ever by his gaze on mine.

"Why did you do this—come all this way—to warn me about Diego?"

Because I love you.

Four simple words. Four simple words that there was

no way I could say. Not to this Jesse, who was virtually a stranger to me. He already thought I was nuts. I didn't want to make things even worse.

"Because it isn't right, what happened to you. That's all."

That's what I started to say, anyway, when a man's voice called, "Señor de Silva?"

And let's just say that it wasn't Mr. O'Neil.

chapter *seventeen*

I felt the blood in my veins run cold.

I knew that voice. Knew it only too well. The man who owned it had tried to kill me once.

"It's him," I whispered. Unnecessarily, of course, since Jesse obviously knew perfectly well who it was.

Jesse stood up and moved from the shadows that had cloaked his face. He wore an expression, I was relieved to see, of intense distrust. He was starting to believe me now.

"Who's there?" he called, lifting the lantern and turning a knob that brought what had been a tiny flame to a more powerful one.

The man below said something in Spanish that I didn't understand. Except for the last two words. And they were easy enough for even me to decipher.

Felix Diego.

This is it, I thought. There was no going back now.

Jesse said something in Spanish to Diego, who replied

in tones that, though I could not understand the words he spoke, sounded too silky-smooth to be trustworthy. He appeared to be inviting Jesse to do something.

And Jesse, for his part, was clearly declining.

"Well?" I whispered anxiously when the conversation ended and I heard Diego finally leave.

Jesse held up a hand, though, clearly not as convinced as I was that the man was well and truly gone.

Then, as the evening turned irrevocably to night and I could no longer see beyond the golden rays shooting out from the lamp Jesse held, he said, "It was Felix Diego. He said his master—Maria's father—had sent him to see that I had everything I needed to be comfortable and to escort me on the remainder of my journey tomorrow."

"Has Maria's father ever done that when you've come to visit before?" I asked.

"No" was Jesse's terse reply to that question.

"What did you tell him?"

"I told him that I was fine," Jesse said. He was answering my questions, but it was clear from the expression on his face that his mind was a thousand miles away. He was putting the extraordinary tales I'd been telling him together with what had just happened, and not liking what he was coming up with.

"I told him I'd be here all night," he went on. "Because my horse was sick. He said my horse looked fine to him and suggested I join him outside for a bottle—"

I sucked in my breath. "You didn't say yes, did you?"

"Of course not." For the first time, Jesse seemed really

to *see* me as he looked at me. "I think you're right. I think he does mean to kill me."

I didn't reply with a hearty *Told you so*, because what would have been the point? Besides, Jesse looked upset enough. Not upset really—stunned. And something else, too. Something I couldn't put my finger on. . . .

At least, not until a second later, when I heard footsteps scrape for a second time on the ladder to the loft. Thinking it was Diego returning, I started toward the ladder, ready to fling the guy's soul back to kingdom come. . . .

But Jesse stepped in front of me, throwing out an arm to stop me from coming any closer.

And I realized what that "something" was that I'd seen in his eye.

But it turned out the person climbing toward us wasn't Felix Diego after all.

"Oh, great," Paul said, when he finally pulled himself up to the top of the ladder and saw us. "Oh, this is just great. What's *he* doing here?" Paul was glaring at Jesse, who glared right back.

"He just found me, Paul," I said. I didn't mention the part where I'd sort of *made* him find me.

Paul just glared at Jesse some more. If he noticed how different Jesse looked alive than he did dead, he didn't exactly mention it.

Jesse, for his part, simply nodded to Paul and asked me, "Is this him? The man who tied you up?"

I should have said no, of course. I should have seen what was coming.

But I didn't think. I just went, "Yeah, that's him."

It wasn't until I saw Jesse's hands clench into fists that I realized what I'd done. "No, wait!" I started to cry.

But it was too late. Jesse had launched himself at Paul like a linebacker, tackling him to the floor of the hayloft, and causing an enormous crash that sent the horses below whinnying and thumping around in their stalls.

"Stop it!" I cried, darting forward and trying separate them.

But it was like trying to pull apart a couple of mountains. Paul, at least, wasn't as into the fight as Jesse was, since I could hear him crying, "Get him off me! Suze, get him *off*—"

On the word *off*, Jesse let go of his own accord and backed away, breathing hard. His shirt had gotten unbuttoned a little in the melee, and I caught a glimpse of his strong hard abs. It was impossible, even given the gravity of the situation, not to appreciate the sight.

"What the—" Paul scrambled up from the hay, brushing bits of it off him. "God, Suze. What did you tell him about me? Doesn't he know *I'm* the good guy here? You're the one who was going to let him get—"

"He knows," I interrupted, quickly.

Paul quit brushing himself and sent me a quizzical look. "He knows?" he echoed. "As in . . . *knows* knows?"

"He knows," I repeated grimly.

"Well," Paul said, looking intrigued. "What brought about that little change of heart? I thought—"

"That was before," I said quickly.

"Before *what*?" Paul found a piece of straw in his hair and pulled it out.

"Before I saw him," I said softly, not looking at either of them.

Paul didn't say anything—which for him was unusual. Jesse, of course, didn't know what we were talking about. He was still mad at Paul for tying me up.

"I don't know if it's considered normal in the time you come from to leave women bound and gagged," Jesse said severely. "But in this day and age, allow me to assure you that such behavior would generally land a gentleman in jail."

Jesse said the word *gentleman* like it was the last thing he actually thought Paul was.

Paul just looked at him. "You know," he said. "I think I like your ghost better."

I felt it wise to change the subject. "He's here," I said to Paul. "Felix Diego, I mean."

"I know," Paul said. "I followed him back here."

"I thought you were going to get rid of him!"

"Yeah, well, I couldn't just walk up to him and suck out his soul in front of everyone."

"Why not?"

"Because I would've gotten shot, that's why not."

"But you could just have shifted back to the future—"

"Uh, and left you tied up in Mrs. O'Neil's hayloft? I don't think so. I'd have had to come back and rescue you." His gaze shifted toward Jesse's. "I didn't know, of course, that Prince Charming here had come along and done it for me."

"So what are we going to do?" I asked. Paul looked at Jesse.

"Well," he said. "What does Wonderboy want to do?"

"Wonderboy?" Jesse glared menacingly in Paul's direction. "Is this person a friend of mine in the future?" he asked me.

"No," I said to Jesse. To Paul I said, "I tried to get him to leave, but he won't go."

Paul looked at Jesse. "Buddy," he said. "I'm not telling you this because I like you. Believe me. But if you stay here, you're gonna get iced. Simple as that. That Diego guy? He means business."

"I'm not afraid of him," Jesse said as if we were morons for not believing him.

"See what I mean?" I said, to Paul.

"Great." Paul sat down on a hay bale, looking pained. "This is just great. So when Diego comes to kill him, he can take a crack at you and me, too."

I opened my mouth to insist this wouldn't happen, but Jesse interrupted.

"If you think I would leave you alone with her again," he said, his gaze never wavering from Paul's face, "you don't know me at all in this future you speak of."

"Don't worry," Paul said, holding up a hand wearily. "I wouldn't expect anything else from you, Jesse. Well, that's it then." Paul leaned back in the hay, making himself more comfortable. "We wait. And if he comes back, thinking you've fallen asleep and he can do the job out here, we take him."

"No." Jesse's jaw was set. He didn't raise his voice. Not at all. His tone was hard as steel, however. "*I* will take him."

"Uh, no offense," Paul said, "but Suze and I, we came here especially just to—"

"I said I'll do it," Jesse said in that same ice-cold voice—the one I had come to recognize as the voice Jesse used only when he was truly angry about something. "I'm the one he's come to kill. I am the one who will stop him."

Paul and I exchanged glances. Then Paul sighed, lifted the horse blanket, and stretched out across the hay in a dark corner of the loft.

"Fine," he said. "Wake me when it's time to shift home."

And to my utter disbelief, he closed his eyes and seemed to doze off.

I glanced at Jesse and saw that he was eyeing Paul with distaste. When he noticed the direction of my gaze, he asked, his tone less hard than before, "You two are friends in the place you come from?"

"Uh," I said. "Not really. More like . . . colleagues. We both have the same . . . gift, I guess you'd call it."

"For traveling through time," Jesse said.

"Yes," I said. "And . . . other things."

"And when I kill Diego"—I noticed he said *when* and not *if*—"you'll go back where you came from?"

"Yes," I said, trying not to think about how incredibly hard that moment was going to be.

"And you want to help me," Jesse said, just as quietly as I'd spoken to him, "because . . . ?"

I realized I hadn't actually answered his question the

first time he'd asked it. In the soft glow of the lamp—he'd turned the flame down to make sure Diego really did think he was sleeping, so he could take him unawares—Jesse had never looked as handsome as he did then. Because, of course, he'd never been alive any other time I'd seen him. His brown eyes looked soft, the lashes around them dark as the shadows all through the loft. His lips—those strong, soft lips that hadn't kissed mine nearly as often as I'd have liked and, in all likelihood, never would again—looked hypnotically appealing. I had to tear my gaze from them and keep it instead on a threadbare spot on the knee of my jeans.

"Because it's what I do," I said, only something was happening in my throat, making the words come out more huskily than I'd intended them to.

I coughed.

"And you do this—" Jesse seemed to mean travel back through time to warn potential murder victims of their impending doom. "—for all who die before their time?"

"Uh, not exactly," I said. "Yours is kind of . . . a special case."

"And are all girls from your time," Jesse went on thoughtfully, apparently not noticing my discomfort or my fascination with his mouth, "like you?"

"Like me? Like . . . that they're mediators?"

"No." Jesse shook his head. "Unafraid, like you. Brave, like you."

I smiled a little ruefully. "I'm not brave, Jesse," I said.

"You're staying here," he said, indicating the loft. "Even

though you know—or think you know—something terrible is going to happen."

"Well, sure," I said. "Because that's the whole reason I came. To make sure it doesn't. Although, to be truthful . . ." I threw a cautious glance at Paul, in case—and he probably was—he was listening. "—really I came here to stop him. Paul, I mean. From stopping Diego. Because you see, if you don't die tonight, you and I—in the future, where I come from—will never meet. And I couldn't bear to let that happen. And you even—in the future—said you didn't want that to happen. Only . . . only . . . here I am, letting it happen. So you see, I'm not brave at all."

I doubt he'd understood a word I'd said. It didn't matter, though. It was as close to an apology as the Jesse I had known and loved was going to get. And I felt I owed him one. An apology. For what I had done.

Which was destroy everything we'd had together.

"I think you're wrong," Jesse said. About my not being brave.

But what did he know about any of it, really?

I just smiled at him.

Which is when I heard it.

chapter *eighteen*

Don't ask me how. I wasn't born with superhearing or anything. I just . . . heard it.

The scrape of the barn door.

And Jesse, over by the ladder, froze. He had heard it, too. A second later, I saw Paul sit up. He hadn't been sleeping. Not at all.

We waited in tense silence, each of us hardly daring to breathe.

Then I heard another scrape. This time, it was of a boot on a ladder rung.

Diego. It had to be. Diego was coming to kill Jesse.

Jesse must have sensed my unease, since he lifted a single hand toward me, palm out, in the universal signal for "Stay." He wanted Paul and me to leave Diego to him.

Yeah. Right.

And then I saw them—Diego's head and shoulders, looming massive and black against the lighter dark of the rest of the barn. His head was turned in the direction of Jesse's supine form—he didn't see anything else.

Slowly, obviously fearful of waking his prey, Diego climbed into the loft, his footfalls softened by all the hay. As he crept closer and closer—now he was five feet away . . . now four . . . now three—I leaned forward, ready to pounce. I had no idea what I was going to do to stop him. He was not a small man, and I'm no black belt. But shifting definitely came to mind.

Paul had his hand on me now, though, holding on to the sleeve of my motorcycle jacket, keeping me back so that Jesse could have a chance at taking care of the problem himself. Funny how in this one thing, Paul should be on Jesse's side, when he'd never taken Jesse's side on any other occasion.

One foot. Diego was now one foot from Jesse's supposedly sleeping form. He reached for something at his waist—his belt. I saw the gleam of his buckle . . . the same buckle that, in my own time, had somehow ended up in the attic. . . .

Then, just as Diego had wrapped both ends of the belt around either fist and yanked the part in the middle taut, to use as a kind of garrote, Jesse's voice, cool and assured, cut through the silence.

In Spanish. He said something in Spanish.

Why? Why had I taken French and not Spanish?

Diego, caught totally off guard, stumbled back a step.

I couldn't stand it.

"What did he say?" I hissed at Paul.

Paul, not looking too happy about playing translator,

said, "He said, 'So it IS true.' Now shut up so I can hear."

Diego recovered nicely, however. He didn't lower the hands that clutched the belt. Instead, he said something.

In *Spanish*.

This time, Paul didn't need any urging.

"He said, 'So you know. Yes, it's true. I'm here to kill you.'"

Jesse said something else. The only word I recognized was a name.

"He said, 'Maria sent you?'"

Diego laughed. Then he nodded. Then he lunged.

I don't think I screamed. I know I sucked in a ton of air and was going to let it out in a shriek. But I found myself holding my breath instead. Because Jesse, instead of rolling out from under Diego, as I would have done, rose up to meet his assailant.

The two men teetered dangerously on the edge of the hayloft floor, just before the twelve-foot drop to the ground below. It was hard to see exactly what was happening in the semidarkness, but one thing was certain: Diego had the advantage, weight-wise.

Now Paul and I were on our feet, completely unnoticed by the two men struggling at the edge of the loft. I tried to rush forward to help, but again Paul wouldn't let me.

"It's a fair fight," he said to me.

But when, a second later, the two men broke apart, and Diego threw aside his belt with a chuckle, I saw that there was nothing fair about the fight at all. Because Diego had suddenly produced a knife. It gleamed wickedly in the light from the lantern, sitting on the loft floor a few feet away from them.

Now the air in my lungs came out in a rush. "Jesse!" I shrieked. "Knife!"

Diego whirled. "Who's there?" he asked in English.

The distraction gave Jesse just enough time to pull from his boot his own knife . . . the one he'd used to cut me loose from Paul's ropes.

"Okay, that's it," I said when I saw this. "Somebody's going to get—"

"That's what we want," Paul said, keeping a firmer grip on me than ever. "So long as it's the right guy."

I couldn't understand what Paul was doing, what he was thinking. Jesse and Diego were circling each other warily now, coming within inches with every other step of the loft ledge. We could stop it. We could stop it so easily. Why wasn't he—

Then it hit me. Was Paul on *Diego's* side? Was this whole thing some kind of weird setup? Had he really failed to find Diego during the day or had he only pretended to go and look for him, so he could have the pleasure of watching Jesse die later? Because that could be the only reason he'd have gone to these elaborate lengths—so that he could watch Jesse die—

I wrenched myself free of him.

"You want Jesse to die," I shrieked at him. "You want him to, don't you?"

Paul looked at me like I was nuts. "Are you kidding? The whole reason I came back was to make sure he didn't."

"Then why aren't you helping him?"

"I don't need—" Jesse ducked as Diego took a swing at him. "—any help!"

"Who are those people?" Diego snarled, lunging at Jesse again.

"No one," Jesse said. "Pay no attention to them. This is between you and me."

"See?" Paul said to me, not without some self-righteousness. "Would you chill?"

But how could I, when I was standing there watching my boyfriend—okay, well, he wasn't exactly my boyfriend, yet—in a struggle for his life? I stood there, my heart in my mouth, barely able to breathe, watching the flash of cold hard metal as the two men circled each other. . . .

And then it happened. Diego suddenly reached behind him, and in a flash had grabbed hold of—

Me.

I was caught so off guard, I couldn't think. All I knew was that one minute I was standing there next to Paul, barely able to watch what was happening, I was so scared . . .

. . . and the next, I was in the middle of it, an arm crushing my throat as Diego held me in front of him, the tip of his silver blade at my neck.

"Drop the knife," he said to Jesse. He was standing so close to me, I could feel his voice reverberating through his body. "Or the girl dies."

I saw Jesse blanch. But he never hesitated. He dropped his knife.

Paul screamed, "Suze! Shift!"

It took me a second to realize what he meant. Diego was touching me. Diego was touching me. All I had to do was picture that hallway I hated so much—that way station between existences—and he and I would both be transported there . . .

. . . and we'd be rid of him forever.

But before I could so much as close my eyes, Diego threw me away from him and lunged at Jesse. I tried to scream as I fell, but my throat was so sore from the force with which he'd held me, nothing came out.

I didn't fall from the loft, however. Instead, I fell against something metal—and glass. Something that broke beneath my weight. Something that soaked the straw beneath me.

Something that burst into flames.

The lantern. I'd fallen on the lantern, and broken it. And set the hay on fire.

The flames broke out more quickly than I ever could have imagined they would. Suddenly, I was separated from the others by a wall of orange. I could see them standing on the other side, Paul staring at me in dumb horror, while Jesse and Diego—

Well, Jesse was trying to keep Diego from plunging a knife into his heart.

"Paul," I shrieked. "Help him! Help Jesse!"

But Paul just stood there looking at me for some reason. It was Jesse who finally broke Diego's grip on him. Jesse who twisted the arm that held the knife until Diego, with a cry of pain, let go of it. And Jesse who hauled off and struck

Diego with a blow to the face that sent him reeling—

Right over the ledge.

I heard his body hit the barn floor, heard the unmistakable snap of breaking bones . . . breaking neck bones.

The horses heard it as well. They whinnied shrilly and kicked at the doors to their stalls. They could smell the smoke.

So, I realized, could the O'Neils. I heard shouts coming from outside the barn.

"You did it," I cried, gazing at a panting Jesse through the smoke and fire. "You killed him!"

"Suze." Paul was still staring at me. "Suze."

"He did it, Paul!" I couldn't believe it. "He's going to live." To Jesse, I said joyfully, "You're going to live!"

Jesse didn't look too happy about it, though. He said, "Susannah. Stay where you are."

Then I saw what he meant. The fire had completely cut me off from the rest of the loft. Even from the ledge. I was cornered by flames. And smoke. Smoke that was getting so thick, I could barely see them.

No wonder Paul had been staring at me. I was caught in a firetrap.

"Suze," Paul said. But his voice sounded faint. Then he cried, "Jesse, no—"

But it was too late. Because the next thing I knew, a large object hurtled at me through the smoke and flame—hit me, as a matter of fact, and knocked me to the ground. It took me a second to realize the object was Jesse and that he'd wrapped himself in the horse blanket I'd slept under the night before. . . .

A horse blanket that was now smoldering.

"Come on," Jesse said, throwing down the blanket, then grabbing my hand and pulling me back to my feet. "We haven't much time."

"Suze!" I heard Paul yelling. I could no longer see him, the smoke was so thick.

"Get down," Jesse yelled to Paul. "Get down and help them with the horses."

But Paul didn't appear to be listening.

"Suze," he yelled. "Shift! Do it now! It's your only chance!"

Jesse had turned and was kicking at the planks that made up the closest wall. The boards shuddered under the assault.

Shift? My mind seemed to be working only murkily, maybe due to all the smoke. But it didn't seem like I could shift just then. What about Jesse? I couldn't leave Jesse. I hadn't gone to all this trouble to save him from Diego just to have him die in a barn fire.

"Suze," Paul yelled once more. "Shift! I'm doing it, too. I'll meet you on the other side!"

Other side? What was he talking about? Was he insane?

Oh, right. He was Paul. Of course he was insane.

I heard a crash. Then Jesse was taking my hand.

"We're going to have to jump," he said, his face very close to mine.

I felt something cool lick my face. Air. Fresh air. I turned my head and saw that Jesse had kicked out enough boards in the barn wall for a person to squeeze through. It was dark through that hole. But lifting my face a little to better feel the deliciously cool breeze, I saw stars in the night sky.

"Do you understand me, Susannah?" Jesse's face was very close to mine. Close enough to kiss me. Why didn't he kiss me? "We'll jump together, on the count of three."

I felt him reach out and grab me by the waist, bringing me close to him. Well, that was better. Much better for kissing—

"One . . . "

I could feel his heart drumming hard against mine. Only how was that possible? Jesse's heart had stopped beating 150 years ago.

"Two . . . "

Hot flames were licking my heels. I was so hot. Why didn't he hurry up and kiss me already?

"Three . . . "

And then we were flying through the air. Not because he was kissing me, I realized. No, because we were really flying through the air.

And as if the fresh cool wind had cleared the smoke from my brain, I realized what was happening. Jesse and I were hurtling toward the ground, which looked extremely far away.

And so I did the only thing I could. I clung to him, closed my eyes, and thought of home.

chapter *nineteen*

I landed with such force, all the wind was knocked out of me. It was like being hit in the back with a railroad tie—which has actually happened to me before, so I would know. I lay there, completely stunned, unable to breathe, unable to move, unable to do anything but be aware of the pain.

Then, slowly, consciousness returned. I could move my legs. This was a good sign. I could move my arms. Also good. Breathing returned—painfully, but there, nonetheless.

Then I heard it.

Crickets.

Not the shrieks of horses as they protested being dragged from their burning stalls. Not the roaring of fire all around me. Not even my own labored breathing.

But crickets, chirping away like they had nothing better to do.

I opened my eyes.

And instead of smoke and fire and burning barn, all I saw were stars, hundreds of them, glowing coldly millions of miles away.

I turned my head.

And saw my house.

Not Mrs. O'Neil's boardinghouse, either. But my house. I was in the backyard. I could see the deck Andy had built. Someone had left the lights on in the hot tub.

Home. I was home.

And I was alive. Barely, but alive.

And I was not alone. Suddenly, someone was kneeling beside me, blocking my view of the hot tub lights, and saying my name.

"Suze? Suze, are you all right?"

Paul was tugging on me, pushing me in places that hurt. I tried to slap his hands away, but he just kept doing it until finally I said, "Paul, quit it!"

"You're okay." He sank down into the grass beside me. His face in the moonlight looked pale. And relieved. "Thank God. You weren't moving before."

"I'm fine," I said.

Then remembered that I wasn't. Because . . . Jesse . . . I had lost Jesse. We had saved him, so that I could lose him forever. Pain—much worse pain than I'd felt during my landing on the cold hard ground—gripped me like a vise.

Jesse. He was gone. Gone for good . . .

Except . . .

Except if that were true, why did I remember him?

I rose up onto my elbows, ignoring the jolt of pain that rose from my ribs when I did so.

That's when I saw him. He was lying on his stomach in the grass a few feet away, totally unmoving, totally not . . .

Glowing.

He wasn't glowing.

I looked at Paul. He blinked back at me.

"I don't know," he said as if the words had been wrung from him. "All right, Suze? I don't know how it happened. You were both here when I showed up just now. I don't know how it happened—"

And then I was on my hands and knees, crawling through the wet grass toward him. I think I was crying. I don't know for sure. All I know was, it was hard to see all of a sudden.

"Jesse!" I reached his side.

It was him. It was really him. The real Jesse, Alive Jesse.

Only he didn't seem too alive just then. I reached out and felt for a pulse on his throat. There was one—my breath caught as I felt it—but it was faint. He was breathing, but barely. I was afraid to touch him, afraid to move him . . .

But more afraid not to.

"Jesse!" I cried, rolling him over and shaking him by the shoulders. "Jesse, it's me, Suze! Wake up. Wake up, Jesse!"

"It's no good, Suze," Paul said. "I already tried. He's there . . . but he's not. Not really."

I had Jesse's head in my arms. I cradled it, looking down at him. In the moonlight, he looked dead.

But he wasn't. He wasn't dead. I'd have known if he was.

"I think we screwed up, Suze," Paul said. "You weren't— you weren't supposed to bring him back."

"I didn't mean to," I said. My voice was so faint, it was practically drowned out by the crickets. "I didn't do it on purpose."

"I know," Paul said. "But . . . I think maybe you need to put him back."

"Put him back where?" I raged. Now my voice was much louder than the crickets. So loud, in fact, that the crickets were startled into silence. "In the middle of that fire?"

"No," Paul said. "I just—I just don't think he can stay here, Suze, and . . . live."

I continued to cradle Jesse's head, thinking furiously. This wasn't fair. No one had warned us about this. Dr. Slaski hadn't said a word. All he'd said was to picture in your head the time and place you wanted to be in, and . . .

And not to touch anything you didn't want to bring through time with you.

I groaned and dropped my face to Jesse's. It was my fault. It was all my fault.

"Suze." Paul reached out and rested a hand on my shoulder. "Let me try. Maybe I can get him back—"

"You can't." I lifted my head, my voice cold as the blade Diego had pressed to my throat. "It'll kill him. He's not like us. He's not a mediator. He's . . . he's human."

Paul shook his head. "Maybe he was meant to die, then, Suze," he said. "Like you said. Maybe we aren't supposed to mess with this stuff, just like you warned me."

"Great." I let out a bitter little laugh. "That's just great, Paul. *Now* you agree with me?"

Paul just stood there, looking anxious. If I could have been capable of feeling anything except despair, at that point, I would have hated him.

But I couldn't. I couldn't hate him. I couldn't think of anything but Jesse. I had not, I told myself, saved him just so I could sit and watch him die.

"Go to the carport," I said in a low, even voice. "And inside the house through the door there. They never remember to lock it. Hanging on a hook by the door are my mom's car keys. Get them and then come back and help me take him to the car."

Paul looked down at me like I was a crazy woman.

"The car?" He sounded dubious. "You're going to . . . drive him somewhere?"

"Yes, you fool," I snarled. "To the hospital."

"The hospital." Paul shook his head. "But Suze—"

"Just do it!"

Paul did it. I know he thought it was futile, but he did it. He got the keys, then came back and helped me carry Jesse to my mom's car. It wasn't easy, but between the two of us, we managed. I'd have dragged him the whole way by myself if I'd had to.

Then we were on the road, Paul driving while I continued to hold Jesse's head in my arms. I didn't think then that what I was doing was futile. Maybe, I kept thinking, the hospital could save him. Medicine had made so many advances in the past 150 years. Why couldn't it save a man who'd just traveled to another time, through another dimension? Why couldn't it?

Except that it couldn't.

Oh, they tried. At the hospital. They came running out with a gurney when Paul went in to tell them we had an unconscious man in the car. They hooked Jesse up to an oxygen mask while the emergency room doctor grilled me. Had he taken drugs? Had too much to drink? Had a seizure? A headache? Complained of pain in his arm?

There was no medical explanation for the coma Jesse was in. That's what the doctor came out and told me, hours later. None that he had been able to determine so far. A CT scan might tell him more. Did I happen to know what kind of insurance Jesse had? His Social Security number, maybe? A phone number for his next of kin?

At 6:00 in the morning, they admitted him. At 7:00, I called my mother, and told her where I was—at the hospital with a friend. At 8:00, I phoned the only person I could think of who might possibly have some idea what to do.

Father Dominic had gotten back from San Francisco the night before. He listened to what I had to say without remark. "Father Dominic, I did . . . I think I did something awful. I didn't mean to, but . . . Jesse's here. The real Jesse. The live one. We're at the hospital. Please come."

He came. When I saw his tall, strong figure approaching the hard plastic seat I'd been sitting in for hours, I nearly collapsed all over again.

But I didn't. I stood up and, a second later, was in his arms.

215

"What did you do?" he kept murmuring over and over. He wasn't talking to just me, either. Paul was there, too. "What did you two do?"

"Something bad," I said, lifting my tear-stained face from his shirt. "But we didn't mean it."

"We were trying to save him," Paul said sheepishly. "His life. We almost did—"

"Until I brought him back," I said. "Oh, Father Dominic—"

He shushed me and went into the room where Jesse lay, so still, the blanket over him barely stirring with each shallow breath. Ghost Jesse, I now realized, would have looked better—more alive—than Alive Jesse did.

Father Dominic crossed himself, he was so startled by what he saw. A nurse was there, taking Jesse's pulse and writing the results down on a clipboard. She smiled sadly when she saw Father Dominic, then left the room.

Father Dominic looked down at Jesse. For the first time, I noticed that the lenses of his glasses were kind of fogged up.

He didn't say anything.

"They want to know what kind of insurance he has," I said bitterly, "before they do more tests."

"I . . . see," Father Dominic said.

"I don't see what more tests are going to tell them," Paul said.

"You don't know," I snapped, lashing out at Paul because I couldn't lash out at the person who most deserved it . . . myself. "Maybe there's something they can do. Maybe there's—"

"Isn't your grandfather here somewhere?" Father Dominic asked Paul.

Paul lifted his gaze from Jesse's unconscious form.

"Yeah," he said. "I mean, yes, sir. I think so."

"Perhaps you should go and pay him a visit." Father Dominic's voice was calm. His presence, I had to admit, was soothing. "If he's conscious, perhaps he'll be able to offer us some advice."

Paul's chin slid out truculently. "He won't talk to me," Paul insisted. "Even if he *is* awake—"

"I think," Father Dominic said quietly, "that if there is a lesson to be learned from all of this, it's that life is fleeting and if there are fences to mend, you had best mend them quickly, before it's too late. Go and make amends with your grandfather."

Paul opened his mouth to protest, but Father Dominic shot him a look that snapped his lips shut. With one final glance at me, Paul left the room, looking aggrieved.

"Don't be too angry with him, Susannah," Father Dominic said. "He thought he was doing right."

I was too tired to argue. Much.

"He thought he was robbing me of Jesse," I said. "Even his memory."

Father Dominic shrugged. "In the end, Susannah, that might actually have been kinder, don't you think? Kinder than this, anyway." He nodded his head at Jesse's unconscious form.

Well, that much was true.

"He would have had to leave, anyway, Susannah,"

Father Dominic said. "Someday."

"I know." The knot in my throat throbbed.

Which was when I remembered. There'd been a ghost in Father Dom's life, as well. The ghost of a girl he'd loved, maybe even as much as I loved Jesse.

"I . . . " I could barely speak, the lump in my throat had swelled to such gigantic proportions. "I'm sorry, Father Dominic. I forgot."

Father Dom just smiled sadly and touched my arm.

"Don't be too hard on him," he said, meaning Paul. Then, with a final glance at Jesse, he said, "There isn't much I can think of to do. But the insurance situation. That I think I can take care of. I'll be back soon. Can I bring you anything? Have you eaten?"

The thought of trying to swallow anything down past the mass in my throat was so ludicrous, I actually laughed a little.

"No, thanks," I said.

"All right." Father Dominic started from the room. At the doorway, however, he paused and looked back.

"I'm sorry, Susannah," he said quietly. "I'm sorry I wasn't there for you when . . . it happened. And I'm more sorry than I can say that it had to end this way."

And with that, he was gone.

I stood there for a moment, not doing anything, not thinking a thing. Then the true meaning of his words sunk in.

And I lost it.

Because Father Dominic was right. This *was* the end. I

could deny it as much as I wanted, but this was it. Jesse was dying, right before my eyes, and there was nothing, nothing on earth, that I could do for him.

And it was *my* fault. My own fault he was leaving me. Sure, I could comfort myself that wherever he was, it had to be better than the half-life he'd had with me.

But that didn't make it hurt any less.

I fell into the chair beside Jesse's hospital bed. I couldn't see, I was crying so hard. Not out loud. I didn't want any nurse to come running with a bunch of tranquilizers or anything. What I really wanted, I realized, was my mom. No, not my mom. My dad. Where was my dad now, when I really needed him?

"Susannah."

I thought about Jesse's grave, the one marked by the headstone Father Dominic and I had paid for. What was in that grave now, if Jesse's body was here? Nothing. It was empty.

But not for long. No, not for long.

"Susannah."

And back in his own time? What were Mr. and Mrs. O'Neil doing right now? Probably combing through the rubble of what had been their barn. They'd find one skeleton for sure. But would they know it wasn't Jesse's? Would Jesse's family have closure or would they wonder forever what had happened to their beloved son and brother?

No. They had no way of knowing the body was Diego's. They'd think it was Jesse. The de Silvas would have a funeral. But for the wrong man.

I felt a hand on my shoulder. Great. Someone was there. Someone was watching me cry my eyes out. Nice. Let the girl have a little time to grieve, would you, please?

"Go away," I snapped, lifting my head. "Can't you see I'm—"

That's when I noticed that the figure beside me was glowing.

chapter *twenty*

I must have jumped about a mile and a half into the air, I was that startled. I know I sprang from the chair, so fast that I knocked it over. I stood there, my chest heaving, my eyes suddenly bone dry, and stared.

Because standing there beside the bed, looking down at Jesse's prone body, was . . .

Jesse.

I looked from one Jesse to the other, not quite believing what I was seeing.

But it was true. There were two Jesses, the dead one and the live one.

Or, I suppose it would have been more correct to say the dead one and the dying one.

"J-Jesse?" I swiped at the tears coating my cheeks with the back of my smoky sleeve.

But Jesse wasn't looking at me. He was staring down at . . . well, at himself, on the bed.

"Susannah," he whispered. "What . . . what did you do?"

I was so overjoyed to see him, I wasn't thinking straight. I went to him and grabbed his hand.

"Jesse, I went. Back through time, I mean," I babbled.

He tore his gaze from the figure on the bed and focused all of that intense dark gaze on me. He didn't look too happy.

"You *went?*" He glared at me. "You went after Slater? After I told you I could take care of myself?"

He was furious. I was so happy to see that fury, however, that I let out a little burble of laughter. I didn't realize, then, what seeing him here in the hospital meant.

"You did take care of yourself," I assured him. "I-I told you—the past you—about Diego, and he didn't kill you, Jesse. You killed him. But then . . . then . . . there was a fire." I swallowed, not feeling like laughing anymore. "In the barn. The O'Neils' barn . . ."

His eyes narrowed.

"The O'Neils," he murmured. He appeared to be in as much of a daze as I was. "I remember them."

"Yes," I said. "There was a fire, and Jesse . . . Jesse, you saved me. Or, at least, you tried to. But . . . but . . ."

My voice trailed off. Jesse had dropped my hand. He was moving closer to the bed, looking down at the body that lay there, barely breathing.

"I don't understand," Jesse said. "How did this happen?"

I bit my lip. There was no time for explanations. Not when, any minute, I knew we were going to have to be saying good-bye . . .

"I did it," I blurted. "I didn't mean to. I meant to save you, Jesse, not . . . not this. But I was still touching you when I shifted back to the future, and you . . . you just got caught."

Jesse finally looked at me like he was really seeing me, maybe for the first time since he'd come into the room.

"You really went back?" He stared at me. "To the past? My past?"

I nodded. What was there to say?

He shook his head. "And Paul? I went to the basilica to look for him, but he was gone. You followed him?"

I nodded again.

"I wanted to stop him," I said. "From . . . from keeping you from dying. But in the end . . . I couldn't, Jesse. It wasn't right. What Diego did to you. I couldn't let it happen again. So I told you. And you killed him. You killed Diego. But then there was the fire and . . . " I looked down at the figure in the bed. I couldn't stifle a sob. "And now I think this is good-bye. I'm sorry, Jesse. I'm so, so sorry."

My vision clouded over again with tears. I couldn't believe any of this was happening. I had always thought of my "gift" as a curse, but never, never had I hated it as much as I did just then. I wished I had never heard of mediators. I wished I had never seen a single ghost. I wished I had never been born.

Then I felt Jesse's hand on my cheek.

"*Querida,*" he said.

He placed his other hand on the bed to balance himself as he leaned across it to kiss me. One last kiss before he was ripped from me forever. I closed my eyes, anticipating the feel of those cool lips against mine. *Good-bye, Jesse. Good-bye.*

His mouth had barely touched mine, however, when I heard him gasp. He jerked his head from mine and looked down.

His hand had touched his living body's leg.

Something seemed to jolt through him, then. He flared more brightly for a second, his gaze on mine more intense than it had ever been in all the time I'd known him.

And then he was sucked down into his body, like smoke pulled into a fan.

And was gone.

Oh his body was still there. But the ghost of Jesse—the ghost I had loved—was gone. In his place was . . .

Nothing. I reached out, desperate to grab some small piece of him, but my hand clutched only air.

Jesse was gone. He was truly gone. He was back inside the body he'd left so long ago . . . the body that, even as I watched, shuddered all over as if to reject the soul that had just entered it. . . .

Then went still as death.

I knew then what had happened. Jesse's body had come forward through time, yes. But not his soul, because two of the same souls could not exist in the same dimension. Jesse's body had been without a soul just as, for so many years, Jesse's soul had been without a body.

Now the two were united at last. . . .

But too late. And now I was going to lose them both.

I don't know how long I must have stood there, holding Jesse's hand, gazing down at him in utter despair. Long enough, I know, that Father Dominic came back, and said, "Don't worry, Susannah, it's all taken care of. Jesse will get the tests he needs."

"It doesn't matter," I murmured, still holding his hand . . . his cold hand.

"Don't give up hope, Susannah," Father Dominic said. "Never give up hope."

I let out a bitter laugh. "And why is that, Father D.?"

"Because it's all we have, you know." He placed a hand on my shoulder. "You did what you did because you loved him, Susannah. You loved him enough to let him go. There's no greater gift you could have given him."

I shook my head, my vision still blurred with tears.

"That's not how it's supposed to go, Father Dominic."

"What's not, Susannah?" he asked gently.

"The saying. It's supposed to be, If you love something, set it free. If it was meant to be, it will come back to you. Don't you know? Haven't you read it?"

When I looked up at Father Dominic to see what he thought of this, I saw that he wasn't even looking at me. He was staring down at Jesse on the bed. Father Dominic's blue eyes, I noticed, were as tear-filled as my own.

"Susannah," he said in a strangled voice. "Look."

I looked. And as I moved my head, I felt the fingers of the hand I was holding suddenly tighten around mine.

Color that hadn't been there a minute before had flooded Jesse's face. His face was no longer the same color as the sheets. His skin was the same olive tone it had been when I'd first seen him, back in the O'Neils' barn.

And that wasn't all. His chest was rising and falling visibly now beneath the blanket that covered him. A pulse thrummed visibly in his neck.

And, as I stood there, staring down at him, his eyelids lifted . . .

. . . and I was falling, as hard as I did every time he looked at me, into the deep dark pools that were Jesse's eyes . . . eyes that weren't just seeing me, but knew me. Knew my soul.

He lifted the hand I wasn't clutching, plucked aside the oxygen mask that had been covering his nose and mouth, and said just one word.

But it was a word that set my heart singing.

"Querida."

chapter *twenty-one*

"Suze!"

I heard my mother's voice calling from downstairs. "Suze!"

I was sitting at my dressing table, admiring my blow-out. CeeCee and I had spent the afternoon getting our hair and nails done. CeeCee hadn't needed a blow-out . . . her white-blonde hair is straight on its own. But she'd gotten an updo, then fretted all afternoon that it wouldn't hold.

My blow-out, however, apparently had staying power, because my hair looked as dark and shimmery as it had when I'd stepped from the salon.

"Suze!" my mom called a third and final time.

I glanced at the clock. I'd made him wait nearly five minutes. That seemed long enough.

"Coming," I yelled and grabbed my evening bag and the filmy white stole that went with my dress.

I went to my bedroom door and threw it open. Coming

up the stairs as I was about to head down them was Jake, carrying a heavy backpack filled with books. From the library.

"Has hell frozen over?" I asked him as he went by me on his way to his room.

"Don't start with me, I've got finals," he growled. Then, just as he was to the door of his room, he turned and, with all apparent sincerity, said, "Nice dress," and disappeared into the confines of his bachelor cave.

I couldn't help smiling. It was the first compliment I'd ever managed to wring from Jake.

I started down the stairs, one hand lifting the hem of my gown. They were the exact same stairs, I realized, as the ones Mrs. O'Neil had chased me down about, oh, 150-something years ago. I wondered if, in my current ensemble, she'd have mistaken me for a hoochie mama. Somehow, I doubted it.

It's nice, I thought, that we have stairs like this. Stairs a girl can really make an entrance on. I got to the last landing, the one that basically served as a stage for girls who were going to their first Winter Formal to pivot and show off their dress to the people waiting in the living room, and paused, preparing to do just that.

But it was no use. I saw that at once. My stepfather was running around with a spoon filled with something green, urging everyone he encountered to taste it, just taste it. My mom was trying to figure out how her new digital camera worked and not doing the world's best job at it. My youngest stepbrother, David, was talking a mile a minute to my date about some new advances in aeronautics he'd seen on the Discovery Channel.

And Max, the family dog, had his nose buried in the front of my date's tuxedo pants.

I guess it was a pretty typical familial scene, one that I'm sure occurs in millions of homes every night.

So why did tears spring to my eyes at the sight of it?

Oh, not at Andy and his spoon, or my mom and her camera, or David and his complete conviction that anyone wanted to hear the entire transcript of the show he'd watched.

No, it was the fact that the family dog kept thrusting his nose into inappropriate places on my date, and that my date had to keep shoving Max away, that made the tears well up.

Because Max could smell my date. Max could finally smell Jesse.

David noticed me standing there on the landing first. His voice trailed off and he dried up, and just stood there staring. After a minute, everyone was staring.

I hastily blinked my tears away. Especially when Max rushed over and tried to thrust his big furry head beneath my skirt.

"Oh, Susie," my mom cooed and to everyone's surprise—especially her own—managed to snap a picture. "You look beautiful."

Andy, spying another victim, raised his spoon toward me, but my mother cut him off at the pass.

"Andy, don't you go near her with that stuff while she's

in that dress," she warned.

That made me smile. When I looked at Jesse, I saw he was smiling, too. A secret smile, just for me—even though now, of course, everyone else could see it, too.

It still took my breath away, same as ever.

"So," I said as casually as I could with a giant lump in my throat. But this one was from joy. "I see you've met Jesse."

Andy summed up their introduction in two words before heading back to the kitchen with his spoon. "He'll do."

My mother was beaming. "So nice to meet you," she said to Jesse. "Now come down here, I want to get your picture together."

I came down the rest of the stairs and went to stand by Jesse's side in front of the fireplace. He looked so tall and handsome in his tux, I could hardly stand it. I didn't even care that my mother was completely mortifying me in front of him. I guess those kind of things don't really matter when you nearly lose your reason for living, then get it back again, against all odds.

"This is for you," Jesse said when I came close enough. He handed me something he'd been holding. It was a single white orchid, the kind you usually only see at funerals. Or on graves.

I took it from him with a wry smile. Only he and I realized the flower's significance. To my mother, who came rushing over to pin it to my dress before she took the picture, it was just a corsage.

"Now, say cheese," she said and took the picture, thankfully without actually making us say it.

Andy reemerged from the kitchen, this time without his spoon, and started looking parental.

"Now, you have her home by midnight, understand, young man?" he said, clearly enjoying being father to a girl instead of a boy for a change.

"I will, sir," Jesse replied.

"One," I said to Andy.

"Twelve thirty," Andy countered.

"Twelve thirty," I agreed. I'd only argued because, well, that's what you do. It didn't really matter what time Jesse had to bring me home by. Not when we had our whole lives together ahead of us.

"Suze," my mom whispered as she fussed with my shawl, "we like him, don't get us wrong. But isn't he a little, well, old for you? After all, he's in college—Jake's age."

If only she knew.

"That makes us about even," I assured her. "Girls mature faster than boys."

Brad chose that moment to come barreling in from the TV room, where he'd been playing video games. When he saw we were still in the doorway, his face twisted with annoyance.

"Haven't you guys left yet?" he demanded and stormed back into the kitchen.

I looked at my mother.

"I see what you mean," she said and patted me on the back. "Have a nice time."

Outside in the crisp evening air, Jesse looked over his shoulder to make sure my parents weren't watching. Then he took my hand.

"Between doing that again and an eternity in hellfire," he said, "I'd take the hellfire."

"Well, you'll never have to do it again," I said with a laugh. "Now that they know you. And besides, they liked you."

"Your mother didn't," Jesse assured me.

"Yes, she did," I said. "She just thinks you're a little old for me."

"If only she knew," Jesse said, voicing, as he so often did, exactly what I'd been thinking.

"Your stepfather, on the other hand, invited me to dinner tomorrow night."

"Sunday dinner?" I was impressed. "He really *must* like you."

We'd reached Jesse's car—well, really, it was Father Dom's car. But Father D. was letting Jesse borrow it for the occasion. Not, of course, that Jesse had a license. Father Dom was still working on getting him a birth certificate . . . and a Social Security card . . . and school transcripts, so he could start applying for colleges and for student loans.

But, the good father had assured us, it wouldn't be hard. "The church," he'd said, "had ways."

"Madam," Jesse said, opening the front passenger door for me.

"Why, thank you," I said, and slid in.

Jesse went around to the driver's seat, slid into it, then

reached for the ignition.

"You're sure you know how to drive one of these things?" I asked him, just to make sure.

"Susannah." Jesse started the engine. "I did not sit idly by eating bonbons for the 150 years I was a ghost. I did make a few observations now and then. And I most definitely know"—he started backing the car out of the driveway—"how to drive."

"Okay. Just checking. Because I could always take over if you need—"

"You will sit where you are," Jesse said, turning onto Pine Crest Drive without nearly hitting the mailbox, which was something even I, a driver with an actual license, rarely managed to do, "and look pretty, as a young lady ought to."

"Wait, which century is this?"

"Humor me," he said, looking pained. "I'm doing it for you, in this monkey suit."

"Penguin."

"Susannah."

"I'm just saying. That's what it's called. You need to get hip with the lingo if you're going to fit in."

"Whatever," Jesse said in such a perfect imitation of—well, me—that I was forced to mock punch him in the arm.

I sat and looked pretty for the entire rest of the two-mile ride to the Mission. When we got there, I even waited and let him come around to open the car door for me. Jesse thanked me, mentioning that his male ego had taken enough blows over the past week.

I knew what he meant and didn't blame him a bit for

feeling that way. He had basically walked out of Carmel Hospital a man newly born, without a past, at least, not one that was going to help him in this century, without family—except for me, of course, and Father Dominic—and without a cent to his name. If it hadn't been for Father Dominic, in fact, who knew what might have happened? Oh, I suppose my mom and Andy might have let him move in with us. . . .

But they wouldn't have been wild about it. But Father Dominic had found Jesse a small—but clean and nice—apartment, and he was looking into a job. College would come later, after Jesse had studied for and taken the SATs.

But when we ran into Father D. at the entrance to the dance—it was being held in the Mission courtyard, which had been transformed for the occasion into a moonlit oasis, complete with white fairy lights twisted around every palm tree and multicolored gels over the lights in the fountain—he pretended he and Jesse were meeting for the first time, for the sake of Sister Ernestine, who was standing nearby.

"Very nice to meet you," Father Dominic said, shaking Jesse's hand.

Jesse was unable to keep a smile from his face. "Same with you, Father," he said.

After Sister Ernestine left with a sniff at my dress—I suppose she'd been waiting for me to show up in something slit to my navel, not the very demure white Jessica McClintock number I was wearing instead—Father Dominic dropped the pretense and said to Jesse, "I have good news. The job's come through."

Jesse looked excited. "Really? What is it? When do I start?"

"Monday morning, and though the pay won't be much, it's something I think you'll be unusually well suited for—giving talks about old Carmel at the Historical Society Museum. Do you think you can stand to do that for a while? Until we can get you into medical school, anyway?"

Jesse's grin seemed—to me, anyway—even more brilliant than the moon.

"I think so," he said.

"Excellent." Father Dominic pushed his glasses up his nose and smiled at us. "Have a nice evening, children."

Jesse and I assured him we would, then went into the dance.

It wasn't any mid-nineteenth-century ball or anything, but it was still very nice. There were punch and cookies and chaperones. And okay, there was also a DJ and a smoke machine, but whatever. Jesse seemed to be enjoying himself, especially when CeeCee and Adam came up to us, and he was able to shake both their hands and say, "I've heard a lot about you both."

Adam, who'd had no idea about Jesse's existence, scowled.

"Can't say I can return the compliment," he said.

But CeeCee, who'd turned pale as her dress when she heard me say Jesse's name, was more friendly. Or at least enthusiastic.

"B-but," she stammered, looking from Jesse's face to mine and then back again, "are—aren't you—"

"Not anymore," I said to her and, though she still looked confused, she smiled.

"Well," she said. Then, more loudly, "Well! That's wonderful!"

That's when I noticed her aunt standing nearby, chatting with Mr. Walden.

"What's she doing here?" I asked CeeCee.

Adam laughed and, before CeeCee could say a word, explained, "Mr. Walden's chaperoning. And guess who he brought as his date?"

"They aren't dating," CeeCee insisted. "They're just friends."

"Right," Adam said with a grin.

"Suze." CeeCee pulled her lace shawl more tightly over her bare shoulders. "Come to the ladies' room with me?"

"I'll be right back," I said to Jesse.

"How—" CeeCee began as soon as she'd dragged me into the ladies'.

But she couldn't get out anything more than that, because a bunch of giggling freshmen came in and crowded around the mirror over the sink, checking their hair.

"I'll tell you someday," I said to her with a laugh.

CeeCee screwed up her face. "Promise?"

"If you'll tell me how it's going with Adam."

CeeCee sighed and checked out her own reflection. "Dreamy," she said. Then looked at me. "It is for you, too. I can tell by your face."

"Dreamy's a good word for it," I said.

"I thought so. Well, come on. No telling what Adam might be saying to him."

We turned to leave just as the bathroom door swung

open, and Kelly Prescott came in. She shot me a supremely dirty look, which I didn't understand until she was followed by Sister Ernestine, who had a measuring tape in her hand. That's when I saw the slit in Kelly's designer gown. It was much higher than the regulation knee-length.

CeeCee and I slipped past the nun and fell giggling into the breezeway.

At least, I was giggling until I saw Paul.

He was standing in the shadows, looking coolly handsome in his tuxedo. He was obviously waiting for Kelly to emerge with her slit adjusted. He straightened when he saw me.

"Uh, tell Jesse I'll be right there, will you, Cee?" I said.

CeeCee nodded and went back to the dance. I walked up to where Paul was leaning against one of the stone pillars, and said, "Hi."

Paul took his hands from his pockets. "Hi," he said.

Then neither of us seemed to be able to think of anything to say.

Finally, Paul said, "I ran into Jesse out there."

I raised my eyebrows."I ran into Kelly in there."

"Yeah," Paul said, flicking a glance at the door to the ladies' room. Then he said, "I . . . my grandfather asked about you."

"Really?" I had heard Dr. Slaski had come home from the hospital. "Is he—"

"He's better," Paul said. "A lot better. And . . . and you were right about him. He isn't crazy. Well, he is, but not in the way I thought. He actually knows a lot of stuff about . . . people like us."

"Yeah," I said. "Well, tell him I said hi."

"I will." Paul looked incredibly uncomfortable. I couldn't blame him, really. It was the first time we'd been alone together since the fire . . . and the hospital. I'd seen him in school the following week, but he'd seemed to do everything possible to avoid me. Now he looked very much like he'd have liked to run away.

But he didn't. Because it turned out he still had something to say.

"Suze. About . . . what happened."

I smiled at him. "It's all right, Paul," I said. "I already know."

He looked confused. "Know? About what?"

"About the money," I said. "The two thousand dollars you donated anonymously to the church's neediest fund, specially earmarked for the Gutierrezes. They got it and, according to Father Dominic, they were deeply grateful."

"Oh," Paul said. And he actually blushed. "Yeah. That. That's not what I meant. What I meant is . . . you . . . you were right."

I blinked at him. "I was? About what?"

"My grandfather." He cleared his throat. I could tell how much it was costing him to admit this. I could also tell, however, that he needed to say it, very badly. "Well, not just about my grandfather, but about . . . well, everything."

I raised my eyebrows. This was more than I'd ever dared hope for.

"Everything?" I echoed, hoping he meant what I thought he meant.

He seemed to. "Yeah. Everything."

"Even about"—I had to be sure—"you and me?"

He nodded, but not very happily.

"I should have known it all along," he said slowly, as if the words were being forced out of him by some unseen force. "How you felt about him, I mean. You told me enough times. But it didn't . . . it didn't really hit me until that night in the barn, when you . . . you told him. Why we were there. The fact that you'd have rather let him live—"

"We don't need to talk about this," I said, because just thinking about that night made my chest feel tight. "Really."

"No," Paul said, his blue-eyed gaze boring into me. "You don't understand. I've got to. I've never—Suze, I've never felt that way about anybody. Not even you. Which you, uh, probably noticed. When I didn't exactly come to your rescue. During the fire and all."

"But you were great afterward," I said, sticking up for him, because I felt like somebody should. "Helping me get Jesse to the hospital and all."

He shrugged miserably. "That was nothing. What Jesse did—jumping through those flames—and he barely even knew you—"

"It's all right, Paul," I said. "Really."

He didn't look convinced. "Really?"

"Really," I said, meaning it. Then I nodded toward the ladies' room door. "Besides, I always thought you two are much better suited, anyway."

"Yeah," Paul said, following my gaze. "I guess."

Then, to my surprise, he stuck out his right hand. "No hard feelings, Simon?"

I looked down at his hand. It seemed incredible, but I really didn't have any. Hard feelings toward him, I mean. Not now. Not anymore.

I slipped my fingers into his.

"No hard feelings," I said.

Then the bathroom door burst open and Kelly came out, her gait considerably altered because Sister Ernestine had stitched the slit in her dress to just above the knee.

Kelly had some pretty unpleasant things to say about the nun as she approached us.

"But at least she didn't make you go home and change," I interrupted her to point out.

Kelly just blinked at me. "Who's that guy?" she wanted to know.

I looked over my shoulder. Jesse was approaching us from down the breezeway. My heart, as always when I saw him, turned over in my chest.

"Oh, him?" I said casually. "That's just Jesse, my boyfriend."

My boyfriend. *My boyfriend.*

Kelly's eyes widened to their limits as Jesse stepped into the pool of moonlight in which we were standing, and took my hand.

"Paul," he said with a nod.

"Hey, Jesse," Paul said, looking uncomfortable. Then, remembering Kelly, he made uneasy introductions.

"Very nice to meet you," Jesse said, shaking Kelly's hand.

She, however, seemed too stunned to reply. She was just staring up at Jesse as if she'd seen . . .

Well, not a ghost, exactly. More like something she couldn't quite understand. I could almost hear her wondering, *What's a guy like* that *doing with* Suze Simon?

Hey, she didn't know what I'd been through for the guy . . . or what he'd been through for me.

Trying not to look too smug, I took Jesse's arm and said, "Well, see you around." And led him to the dance floor.

"Things with Paul are . . . ?" Jesse raised his eyebrows questioningly as I slid my arms around his neck.

"Fine," I said.

"And you know that because . . . ?"

"He told me."

"And you believe him?"

"You know what?" I lifted my head from where I'd been resting it on Jesse's shoulder. "I do."

"I see." Jesse stood there as I swayed to the music. "Susannah? What are you doing?"

"I'm dancing with you."

Jesse looked down at our feet, but couldn't see them, because my long skirt was swaying above them.

"I don't know this dance," he said.

"It's easy," I said. I let go of his neck and took his hands and brought them around my waist. Then I put my arms back around his neck. "Now sway."

Jesse swayed.

"See?" I said. "You're doing it."

Jesse's voice in my ear sounded a bit strangled. "What's

this dance called?" he asked.

"Slow," I said. "It's called a slow dance."

Jesse didn't say anything much after that. He really was catching on fast to twenty-first-century social customs.

I don't know how much later it was that I lifted my head and saw my dad standing there.

This time, I didn't jump out of my skin. I'd sort of been expecting to see him.

"Hey, kiddo," he said.

I stopped dancing and said to Jesse, "Could you just excuse me a minute? There's just somebody I have to, um, have a word with."

Jesse smiled. "Of course."

My heart swelling with adoration for him, I hurried over to the palm tree my dad was lurking behind.

"Hey," I said to him, a little breathlessly. "You came."

"Of course I came," Dad said. "My little girl's first real dance? You think I'd miss it?"

"That's not why I'm glad you came," I said, reaching out to take his hand. "I wanted to say thanks."

"Thanks?" Dad looked bewildered. "For what?"

"For what you did for Jesse."

"For Jesse?" Then comprehension dawned and he made as if to drop my hand, looking embarrassed. "Oh. That."

"Yes, *that*," I said, holding his fingers more tightly. "Dad, Jesse told me. If you hadn't made him come to the hospital when you did, I'd have lost him forever."

"Well," he said, looking as if he wished he were some-place—anyplace—else. In fact, he looked . . . well, almost as if he already *were* someplace else. He was much less opaque than usual. "I mean, you were crying. And calling me. When it was Jesse you should have been calling."

"I thought Jesse was gone," I said. "So I called you. Because you've always been there when I really needed you. And you were there for me then, too. You saved him, Dad. And I just wanted to let you know how much that meant to me. Especially since I know you didn't agree with my going—you know—in the first place."

My dad reached up to straighten my orchid. But for some reason, instead of being able to grab onto it, his fingers seemed to go right through the waxy petals. Suddenly, I realized what was happening. And there was nothing I could do but stand there, looking up at him, tears gathering beneath my eyelids.

"Yeah, sorry about that," Dad went on, meaning our disagreement about my going back through time to "save" Jesse. He was growing physically fainter and fainter with every word. And it wasn't just because I was looking at him through a veil of tears. "It's just that if you'd gone back and saved my life, it would have been like . . . well, like I'd died—and been hanging around for the past ten years for nothing."

"It wasn't for nothing, Dad," I said, holding as tightly as I could to the hand that, even as I spoke, I could feel slipping away. "It was for Jesse. And for me. That's why you're finally ready to move on. See for yourself."

Dad looked down at himself and then at me, clearly stunned.

"It's okay, Dad," I said, reaching up with my free hand to wipe the tears from my face.

He was almost impossible to see now . . . just a shimmer of color and light, and a faint pressure on my hand. But I could tell he was grinning. Grinning and crying at the same time. Just like I was. "I'll miss you."

"Take care of your mother for me," he said quickly, as if he were afraid of being snatched away before he could get the words out.

"I will," I promised.

"And be good," he said.

"Am I ever anything but?" I asked, my voice breaking.

Then, with a shimmer, he disappeared.

Forever.

It was a long time before I could go back to where Jesse was standing. I'd had to cry for a while behind one of the palm trees, then repair the damage those tears had done with the makeup from my bag. When I finally returned to Jesse's side, he looked down at me, and smiled.

"He's gone?" he asked.

"He's gone," I said automatically. Then I gasped.

"Jesse . . ." I stared up at him. "Can you . . . did you. . . ?"

"See you talking to your father just then?" he asked, the corners of his lips twitching a little. "Yes."

"Then you can . . ." I was completely dumbfounded. "You can . . ."

"See and speak to ghosts?" Jesse grinned in the moonlight. "Apparently so. Why? Is that a problem?"

"No. Except that . . . that would mean—" I could barely

believe what I was saying. "That means you're a—"

"*Querida*," Jesse said, pulling me toward him. "Let's just dance."

But I was still too stunned to think of anything else. Jesse—my Jesse—was no longer a ghost. He was a mediator.

Like me.

"The only thing I don't understand," Jesse was saying, his breath warm in my ear, "is why it took him all this time."

I swayed in Jesse's arms, barely registering what he was saying. *Jesse is a mediator*, was all I could think. *Jesse's a mediator now.*

"Your father," Jesse said. "His moving on, I mean. Why now?"

I put my arms around his neck. What else could I do?

"Do you really not know?" I asked him.

He shook his head.

I smiled because I felt as if my heart might burst with joy.